BEAR ATTRACTION

SHIFTERS UNBOUND
BOOK 6.5

JENNIFER ASHLEY

JA / AG PUBLISHING

Bear Attraction

Shifters Unbound Book 6.5

Copyright © 2015 by Jennifer Ashley

This book is a work of fiction. The names, characters, places, and incidents are products of the writer's imagination or have been used fictitiously and are not to be construed as real. Any resemblance to persons, living or dead, actual events, locales or organizations is entirely coincidental.

All Rights are Reserved. No part of this book may be used or reproduced in any manner whatsoever without written permission from the author. Nor is this book to be used to train AI databases.

Cover design by Kim Killion

CHAPTER ONE

Rebecca could still hear the hunters with guns behind her. *Assholes.* They'd come out here to take potshots at rabbits, but decided that the Kodiak bear they'd spotted would make a much better trophy.

Rebecca—the Kodiak in question—sprinted across a stretch of broken pavement that had once been a runway and back into the tall grasses and weeds. In the summer, this field would be lush with sunflowers. Now, in October, dry grasses crackled under her paws in the darkness.

More changes had occurred since this summer—Austin's old airport was plowed up more every day to build condos and office complexes, which sprang up like fungi. Rebecca skirted a huge pile of upturned earth and chunks of asphalt, and kept running.

Even with the encroachment, these wide-open, flat fields were the best place in town for a Shifter bear to run, especially at night. Rebecca came out here several times a week to run off her frustrations, her hormones, or whatever, and just to be alone under the sky. On clear nights, the stars stretched to infinity, a blush of white against deep black.

She could pretend she was in Alaska again, where she might go for days without seeing a human, or even another bear, wild or otherwise. It had taken her forever to get used to living not only in a city but crammed into Shiftertown with other Shifters. Where she'd once existed in complete solitude, she now shared a house with another Kodiak of her clan, his human mate, and four assorted cubs, three of them fosters.

Rebecca had come to love them all, but sometimes, she needed to escape out here to run in the silence and the stillness.

"Got 'im!" one of the men behind her yelled.

So much for stillness. The men chasing her weren't real hunters—just a bunch of stupid guys with too much firepower and too few brains.

They had no idea Rebecca was a she, not a he, and a Shifter, not a wild bear. They didn't care. They were going to shoot her and drag her home, no matter what.

Rebecca's advantage was that she knew this place like the back of her paw. She ran and dodged, finding the sudden valleys in what seemed a level, smooth plain. She felt grim satisfaction when one of the hunters yelled, "Damn, where'd he go?"

The thought *What is a Kodiak bear doing running around the old airport?* apparently never crossed their minds. These were the kind of guys who saw something moving and tried to shoot it. Their mothers must be so proud.

Rebecca ran through a drainage ditch, dry from lack of rain, and angled back toward Shiftertown, which lay a little north of the airport, in an older area bounded by Airport Boulevard. The bungalows there were similar to others in hidden neighborhoods around it, historic places developers hadn't gone after yet.

Once Rebecca made it closer to Shiftertown, the hunters would have to give up. She'd hit busier roads, plus the Shifter trackers who patrolled the perimeter would make sure Rebecca got safely home.

Of course, Rebecca had to make it inside the perimeter first. She had about a half mile to go, and there were five hunters out here with her.

She dashed up out of the ditch, ready to sprint the last stretch back to Shiftertown . . . and almost landed on top of one of the hunters.

He yelled, "*Shhhh-iii-t!*" and rolled backwards, desperately clutching his gun. Rebecca didn't give him a chance to shake off his terror. She pounced.

A couple thousand pounds of Kodiak coming down on him had to be a fearsome sight. The man scrambled out of the way and to his feet, screaming for his friends. Rebecca reached him in another stride and knocked his shotgun from his hands with her massive front paw. She scooped up the gun and rose on her hind legs, a Kodiak at its mightiest.

Her bear paws could manipulate things pretty well, and in a few seconds, she had the rifle uncocked and broken in half. The man she'd taken it from gibbered for a second, then turned and ran.

Rebecca dropped to all fours and ran in the opposite direction. But too late, the man's friends had surrounded her, fear on their faces but rifles and shotguns raised. One trained a powerful lantern flashlight on her.

Rebecca had several choices, including shifting back to human to show him she wasn't a wild bear. But that was risky—while Rebecca could be stronger than most human men, there were five of them, and they'd probably be delighted to find a naked woman among them. No telling what they'd try to do then.

She could run, dive into darkness and try to lose them with sheer speed and cunning. Or she could fight.

Rebecca rose on her hind feet, her ruff high. She spread her front paws, giant things the size of dinner plates, and roared. The sound shook the ground.

The men shouted, swore—one even laughed with the hysterical laughter of the truly terrified. A couple of them ran. One fired.

Rebecca's reflexes made her dive aside, but buckshot grazed her side, hurting. Her frenzy grew, her human thoughts scattering as her bear instincts took over. Rebecca roared again, came down on all fours, and charged.

The men streamed outward like a startled flock of birds. Rebecca picked one at random, and gave chase.

The hunter sprinted away, forgetting about the gun in his hands, but he'd never be able to outrun Rebecca. She'd land on him, break his shotgun, flip his body back and forth between her paws—generally scare the crap out of him. Maybe she'd close her big teeth around his neck, tasting his fear. Something inside her told her she couldn't kill him— she'd be executed for it—but that didn't mean her bear couldn't have a little fun.

Rebecca closed on the man as he panted in fear, invoking his deity with every breath. One more stride . . .

The hunter charged past another man, who was standing

still, at first just one more patch of darkness. Moonlight glinted on the newcomer's white-blond hair and the barrel of the rifle he aimed at Rebecca.

Not a shotgun—a tranq rifle. Behind him stood more men dressed in black, holding real guns, ready to shoot.

"Stand down," the lead man said to Rebecca. He had no fear in his voice; he expected to be obeyed.

Rebecca skidded to a halt, her paws tearing up dirt and grass. She let the other human go—lesser prey. The man with the tranq rifle—now *he* pissed her off.

She rose up on her hind feet, growling, ready to grab the rifle out of his hands.

"Rebecca," the man said in a calm voice. "There's enough tranq in here to put you out for the rest of the night. You can either come with me on your own, or be dragged away by my men."

Rebecca growled again, the sound rumbling through her body. Only one thing she could do in a situation like this.

She stretched to her full height, then she let herself slowly melt into her human form, fur receding and vanishing as her limbs changed. Her muzzle flattened, her face became human, and her paws became long-fingered human hands.

She would be stark naked when she finished shifting, but that was his problem, not hers.

Rebecca's bear body finally vanished, and she shook herself out, her skin tingling from the shift. She put her hands on her hips, cocking her head so that her Collar caught the light.

"Walker Danielson," she drawled. "What brings you out here in the middle of the night?"

———

If Rebecca had one weapon that could completely disarm Walker, it was this—standing naked in front of him, moonlight kissing her body.

Darkness hid most of her, but silver light touched her breasts, pale skin with dark areolas, her rich brown hair, and a smile he could never forget. The moonlight also glinted on her Collar, marking her as a Shifter and a captive.

"*You* bring me out here," Walker said, not lowering the tranq gun. "I heard report of a bear running around the old airport."

He knew the tranq rifle didn't intimidate her. She could morph back into a bear the second she wanted to and take him down.

Walker had a vivid memory of lying on her living room carpet, while Rebecca as a giant bear stretched across his chest. She'd held him better than manacles. He hadn't been able to move, barely able to breathe.

Rebecca hadn't crushed or smothered him. She'd been gentle, holding him in place, only letting him up without a scratch when her roommate, Ronan, had come to chain him up. That had been Rebecca being nice, following Ronan's orders. What she'd do now, out here alone in the night, was anyone's guess.

"And naturally you thought of me," Rebecca said, one hip canted. "I'm flattered."

As always, Walker's throat closed up when she turned on her full power. Words didn't come easily to him at the best of times, and he had to struggle now to speak evenly.

"Developers aren't happy about people running around their new buildings. They have tight security."

"When you say *people*, you mean *Shifters*." Rebecca started toward him, her body swaying in the darkness. Walker's finger sweated on the trigger. "Those *human* idiots were out here to shoot at rabbits. With big guns, so they could hear them go *boom*."

She kept coming. Walker stood his ground. Rebecca didn't believe he'd tranq her, not when she was in human form, naked and sexy. She was wrong.

The first time they'd met, Walker had been trying to free himself, and he'd worried about hurting the gorgeous woman left to guard him. He'd fought her, throwing her off, and while he'd hesitated, concerned after she'd slammed into the staircase, she'd climbed to her feet and stripped out of her clothes.

Instead of taking the moment to run, Walker had allowed himself to get distracted by her amazing body. He'd given her time to turn into a bear and pin him down.

Not this time. "I won't shoot you if you walk away with me now," Walker said, watching her through the gun's scope.

"To do that, I need my clothes. Which I left over there." Rebecca pointed one long finger off into the darkness. The gesture made her breasts move, and Walker kept sweating. "You think those hunters will leave me alone now that I'm a naked woman?"

"Don't make me arrest you, Rebecca."

"For what?" Her hand returned to her hip. "Having a run? By myself? The rabbits are safe from me."

"For trespassing. The security companies out here mean serious business."

"In other words, they don't like Shifters."

"They don't like *anyone*. Come with me, and they won't press charges."

"Are you going to make me?" Rebecca's voice went sultry. She could turn it on, this woman, and leave Walker aching all night. "You and whose army?"

"The platoon standing behind me. They have lights, tranq guns and other guns, and an armored Humvee."

"Seriously?" Rebecca peered into the darkness. "All that for little ole me?" She sniffed. "I don't smell anything."

"They're trained to cover scent. They're experienced at tracking down Shifters."

"Are you trying to scare me, Captain Danielson?" She resumed her slow stalk and her sexy voice.

"Major." Walker cleared his throat. "Major Danielson now."

"Oh, that's right. How nice."

She kept coming. Walker had to remind himself about twenty times that though she might be the sexiest woman alive, she was dangerous as hell, never mind the shock Collar around her neck.

Walker's body wouldn't manifest the right reaction. He should be wanting to fight the threat or flee from it. Instead, his instincts were telling him to throw down the rifle, grab Rebecca, haul her into his arms, and kiss the hell out of her.

His training kept him in a defensive stance, rifle raised. He hadn't survived all this time in the most dangerous parts of the world by letting his hormones take over. Walker had learned to focus, to channel his energy into defeating the enemy, whether that might be crazed men trying to kill him in remote mountains or a beautiful Shifter smiling at him in the dark.

"Five seconds," Walker said. "You stand there and let me escort you out, or I tranq you. Your choice."

"Yeah? How about we talk about it? Just you and me?" Rebecca smiled—her warm smile that said she was large-hearted, friendly, and great in bed. She took another step toward him.

Walker knew what he had to do next. The decision was tough, but it was out of his hands.

He relaxed and lowered the tranq gun. "All right."

Just like that, Rebecca was bear. The Kodiak snarled, ruff high, and came at him with giant paws, ready to battle.

Except Walker's tranq dart was in her side. He'd lifted the rifle and fired as soon as she'd started to shift.

The bear's eyes widened as the fast-acting tranq coursed through her body. She growled, her eyes going flat, and Walker knew exactly what she was saying.

You bastard.

Rebecca fell to the ground with a resounding thud. Ten men came out of the darkness to surround the bear whose sides now rose and fell in peaceful sleep.

CHAPTER TWO

R ebecca groaned as consciousness returned. She hurt—a sharp pain stabbed her in the side and a dull one danced around her abdomen. Her back hurt too, her usually comfortable bed for some reason too hard. Or maybe she'd fallen asleep on the floor.

Didn't matter, she had to get up and fix breakfast for the cubs. She and Elizabeth traded off the cooking, and today was her day.

Or maybe they'd already had breakfast. She couldn't remember.

Rebecca peeled open her eyes . . . and sat up fast.

She was in a cramped, dingy room with a large steel door and no windows. A small square opening in the door was covered with bars. Rebecca sat on a slab built into the wall, dressed in what looked like a hospital gown.

When she tried to scramble to her feet, she found she was also shackled by one wrist to the wall.

"Seriously?" she yelled.

She heard the beeping of a keypad, then the door clicked open. The door was clean, solid, and new, unlike the rest of the cell, which was shabby and worn, walls and floor pitted.

Major Walker Danielson strode in. He was minus the tranq rifle—he wasn't armed at all that Rebecca could see. He wore black fatigues, the gold leaf that was his major's insignia adorning one shoulder, another insignia she didn't recognize on the other. The tag above his right pocket, in olive green so it could be seen among the black, read "Danielson."

Walker let the door close behind him, shutting himself in with her. The *snick* of it told her the electronic lock had clicked into place.

Rebecca remained on the bunk, hands bracing herself at her sides. Did he expect her to jump to attention? Salute? What?

Walker said nothing. He was a man of few words; she already knew that. He was also tight-bodied and exuded incredible strength, a fact Rebecca had been aware of the first time she'd seen him.

His eyes were light blue in a face tanned from years of working in the sun. His hair, which he kept in a buzz, was a sun-streaked blond. The backs of his hands were scarred, as were his arms, a man who'd fought and fought often.

Right now, his arms were covered by the sleeves of his fatigues, and he'd folded them across his chest. Not a welcoming stance. A delicious-looking man, but one who took no shit.

Rebecca was an unmated Shifter female in her prime years, and her frenzy was never far from the surface. Walker was a fine and virile man, and though she was his captive, his physical presence did things to her.

But if she went into mating frenzy here and now, she'd be tranqued again, and the Goddess only knew where she'd wake up next time. She'd have to suppress her biological urges, at least long enough to figure out what was going on and get back home.

She wet her dry mouth before she could speak. "What the hell am I doing here?" she croaked. "I feel like shit. *What* was in that tranq?"

"You'd been shot by the hunters," Walker said, his voice irritatingly calm. "We took some shot out of you while you were out. The tranq will wear off. It's harmless to you."

"Harmless? Right. Because you're so up on how Shifter metabolisms work."

Walker didn't change expression. "I work for Shifter Bureau. They know all kinds of things about Shifters and their metabolisms."

"Yeah, from all those experiments." Twenty years ago, when Shifters had first come out, Shifter Bureau had rounded up many Shifters and stuck them into labs to see how they worked.

"We still have the information." Walker let out a short breath, the military man at last cracking to reveal the human beneath. "Rebecca, they ordered me to bring you in. The developers were making a stink about a Shifter running around on their land—one developer in particular, who has a lot of weight."

"Maybe he should go on a diet." Rebecca wet her mouth again, a sour scratch in her throat. She wanted water. Or beer. Beer would be better.

"They're building a research facility," Walker said. "Big pharma. Lots of money, very powerful. Theft is a huge deal for them, and they're not happy that so many Shifters live nearby."

"Then why the hell did they buy land next to Shifter-town?" Rebecca snapped. "What did they expect?"

"They're good with it if Shifters stay away from their property and buildings. Their area is clearly marked, and they have plenty of security to keep an eye on things." Walker pinned her with his gaze. "You ran right through the site."

"I was being chased by stupid human drunks with guns. Why wasn't security all over *their* asses?"

"They were. The police responded to that call. I got the one about you."

"Lucky you." Rebecca lifted her hand to move her hair from her face, but she was brought up short by the chain. "What's up with this? I could turn bear and yank it out with one pull."

"You might not want to do that," Walker said. "It's shock triggered, like your Collar. It will hurt, maybe knock you out again."

Rebecca lowered her hand in disgust. "Gee, you thought of everything."

"Procedure. By the book."

"There's a book on how to confine Shifters?" Rebecca raked her hair back from her face, being careful to use her free hand. "No. Wait. Of course there is." Her rage was a low simmer, her body too tired to let it boil over.

Walker had originally been assigned to the military attachment to Shifter Bureau, but in the last couple months, he'd pretty much taken over as a liaison between the bureau and Shiftertown. He now worked with a Shifter called Tiger training humans and other Shifters in search-and-rescue operations.

Walker had become a strong voice advocating for the equal treatment of Shifters. And yet, here Rebecca was, tranqued, chained, locked in . . .

"I thought you were supposed to be on *our* side," she said.

"I am." Walker leaned against the wall, completing the illusion of him being relaxed and friendly. Rebecca knew better—his scent broadcast that he was plenty tense.

"Sure, I can tell. What did Liam say when you told him you'd imprisoned me? Or have you called him yet?"

Liam Morrissey was Shiftertown leader. Walker was supposed run everything Shifter related past him.

"Liam understands," Walker said. "He knew I had to do what I had to do. If I hadn't, you might now be in a termination cell. These guys aren't messing around, Becks."

Rebecca winced as he used her pet name. Only Ronan and the cubs called her that, but Walker had heard it from them.

"Fine, you made your point." Rebecca tried to look contrite. "I'd like to go home now. Olaf gets upset if I'm not in by a certain time every night. You wouldn't want to frighten a cute widdle polar bear cub, now, would you?" She blinked soft eyes at him.

Walker didn't look impressed. "Olaf is fine. I talked to Ronan. And it's nine o'clock in the morning."

Which meant she'd been here all night. "Shit."

"I can't let you go yet," Walker said. "Shifter Bureau is

not happy with you. They had to talk fast to the pharma company to have you released to me."

Rebecca groaned, sore all over. "All I did was go for a run, for the Goddess's sake. What's next? We're not allowed to breathe or take a crap?"

Walker shrugged, moving his shirt across tight shoulders. "What I'm thinking is there's something the company plans to do in that building that's valuable. Maybe billions valuable. Corporations are paranoid. They complained to Shifter Bureau, and Shifter Bureau's taking it out on you."

"Great."

Rebecca drew a breath, trying to still her shakes. She didn't want Walker to see she was scared. She didn't fear much, but no one ever knew what crazy stupid thing Shifter Bureau might take into their heads to do to Shifters.

"So, what now?" she asked. "They're going to put me in a special cage and throw away the key? Or do I get to stay in *this* luxurious accommodation?"

She spoke lightly, but dread bit her. Being confined was one of Rebecca's greatest fears, the one she'd had to fight hardest when she'd been moved to Shiftertown. She'd learned how to survive and even like living with others, but part of the reason she'd been able to was that she'd go out running whenever she got too squirrelly. The thought of being kept in a jail like this made her panic rise.

"I've talked them into letting you go home," Walker said. "As long as you stay the hell away from the old airport . . . and help me out with an assignment."

Rebecca didn't hear anything past *letting you go home.* Her heart lifted. She wouldn't have to stay confined. She was going home. She'd hug everyone when she got there, from the giant Ronan to small Olaf to the tiny Coby, Ronan's cub.

"You all right with that?" Walker asked. "I have a bunch of forms for you to sign, and then we're good to go, with you under my custody."

Rebecca snapped out of her daydream of a joyous group hug. "Wait . . . *What?* Your *custody?*"

Walker was back to being the tight-ass officer. "Shifter Bureau is letting you go but only under my supervision. I'll be responsible for your good behavior."

Rebecca stared at him in shock. "Holy shit. For how long?"

"Until they decide. Probably until I clear up the mess there and prove that you helped me."

"Mess?" Rebecca's brain was trying to catch up.

"The woman, Joanne Greene, accused Shifters of abducting her sister this past summer—the sister still hasn't been found."

"Yeah, I know Joanne. She's gotten close to Broderick, of all people." Broderick was a shithead of a Lupine, thought he was the big, bad wolf. "Joanne has changed her mind that our Shifters took her sister," Rebecca went on.

"Yes, but the sister is still missing. I've been assigned to clear up the case, and I need Shifter help to do it. You just volunteered."

Rebecca suppressed a growl. She wanted to shift, but if she did, fifty men might burst in and pop tranqs into her, not to mention the shock cuff locked around her wrist would go off. "All right, fine. Here's my help—I can guarantee you that Shifters had nothing to do with her disappearance. There. Can I go home now?"

Walker gave her a hint of a smile, which made his blue eyes sparkle. "Nope. You need to be processed, then I drive you back."

"*Processed*. Why don't I like the sound of that?"

"It just means going through a bunch of paperwork. And a physical, to make sure they don't have to quarantine you."

Quarantine. Another word to make her shudder. "Oh, for fuck's sake. Shifters are never sick. And I don't have fleas." Rebecca lifted her arms from her sides to show him she was flea free.

Steel returned to Walker's voice. "Just do it, Rebecca. They're looking to take out their embarrassment on someone, and you're right in front of them. Do what I tell you, keep your mouth shut, and you'll be out of here today. Give them shit, and they might just put you in a cage for a year."

Fear of that, far more than Walker's tone, made Rebecca back down. "Fine. Whatever. Give me the paperwork. And some clothes, please?" She clenched her left fist. "You'll have to release me from this to sign anything. I'm left-handed."

Walker shot her a look. "No, you're not. Your file says you're right-handed. Which is why I told them to chain up your left."

"*You* told them? Thanks a lot."

"They were going to chain both," Walker said quietly. "I convinced them that one was enough." He pushed himself off the wall. "First paperwork, then you get clothes."

He started for the door. In a moment, he'd be on the other side of it, leaving Rebecca in solitude, but locked in, trapped. Sweat trickled down her spine.

"Walker," she said quickly.

He turned back, the dim light from the hall burnishing his hair and the diamond blue gray of his eyes.

Rebecca swallowed. "Thank you. For helping me."

"Don't thank me yet, sweetheart," Walker said. "Let's get you out of here first."

He opened the door and slipped out, fast enough that even if she was able to yank free of the shackle, she'd never reach the door before it closed.

The steel door banged, the echo of the lock clicking. Rebecca pulled her feet up under her and scrunched into a ball, the bear in her howling like a pitiful cub.

CHAPTER THREE

By the time Walker was able to get all the paperwork done and Rebecca out of there, it was already late afternoon, the sky darkening.

Walker drove to Shiftertown in his black 250, Rebecca next to him in a set of clean sweats borrowed from one of his sergeants. Rebecca had her arms folded, sitting as far from Walker as she could get.

This incident was regrettable, because Walker had thought, since he'd begun working with Tiger, that Rebecca had softened to him. That they'd started to be friends.

Now Rebecca turned her head and stared firmly out the window, wanting nothing to do with him. Neither said a word on the drive back through town, not even when Walker turned onto the narrow streets of Shiftertown.

It was dark, but many Shifters were out, enjoying the mild October evening. Walker had grown to like coming to Shiftertown, the community of it reminding him that there was more to life than work. The bungalows were old but well kept, yards spilling into yards, gardens neat and blooming, even this late in the year. Shifter cubs played together on patches of grass, watched over by adults from porches. Or from trees, depending on what kind of Shifters the parents were.

Rebecca lived in a house that was bigger than many of the small bungalows that lined the curving roads. Kodiak bears took up a lot of space. Ronan, her roommate, had paired up with a human woman, Elizabeth, last year, and earlier this year, their firstborn had joined them. Ronan and Rebecca had previously taken in three foster cubs, filling up the house.

They called them "cubs," but two of them, Scott and Cherie, were old enough to be adults in human terms. Cherie was twenty-one, Scott, twenty-nine and almost through what Shifters called the *Transition*, which was the change from cub to adulthood. The Transition was similar to puberty for humans, but fifty times as dangerous. The chain in the dining room that had held Walker to the wall this summer had been put there for Scott.

Walker pulled into the house's long driveway, parking next to two Harleys and a small pickup. The two-car garage behind the house had been enclosed, giving the family extra living space they called the Den. The house itself was two stories, large and airy. Everything about this place was big.

Except for the small boy who came charging from the porch to fling his arms around Rebecca's legs as soon as she got herself out of the truck. Rebecca leaned down and lifted the white-haired, black-eyed boy, holding him close.

"I'm all right," Walker heard her say in soothing tones. "I'm all right, Olaf. See?"

The boy with the too-serious expression touched Rebecca's face. "Scott said you weren't coming back. He said they would kill you."

"Well, Scott was wrong," Rebecca said firmly. "I wasn't going to let them."

"I told him that," Olaf declared. He threw his arms around Rebecca's neck and smacked a kiss to her cheek.

Without looking at Walker, Rebecca started for the house, still carrying Olaf. Olaf was ten, and getting leggy, but he looked younger in tall Rebecca's arms.

Walker slung his duffel bag over his shoulder and followed them without a word.

The front door was already open, the family surging onto the wide front porch to surround Rebecca as she set Olaf on his feet. Ronan, the big, heavily muscled man who worked as a bouncer, enfolded Rebecca in a body-swallowing hug.

"You okay, Becks?" he asked.

Rebecca nodded, her black hair glistening under the porch lights. Ronan pulled her close, hands on her back. There was nothing sexual in the hug—it was a wordless show of support, telling her she wasn't alone. Rebecca wiped tears from her eyes when Ronan released her, and gave him a nod and a little smile.

Once Ronan stepped away from Rebecca, the others rushed her. Elizabeth, a small woman with blue streaks in her hair, had to stand on tiptoe to get her arms around Rebecca, who bent down for her. Cherie hugged Rebecca tightly from the other side, and lanky Scott wrapped wiry arms around her from behind.

Rebecca hugged, kissed cheeks, smoothed hair, and finally said, "All right, all right. You're going to knock me over, and I'm so tired I'll pass right out. If I sleep on the porch floor all night, I'll be cranky in the morning."

Laughter, strained but relieved, followed. They let her go after Cherie gave Rebecca one last hug.

Olaf had stood off to the side, seeming to take comfort from watching the others comforting one another. He turned his head and regarded Walker with steady dark eyes.

"Thanks for bringing her home, Walker," he said in his small voice that held a hint of gruff bear. He looked pointedly at the duffel bag over Walker's shoulder. "Are you spending the night?"

"Yes," Rebecca said. "He's been assigned to be my babysitter."

Ronan, head of the household, fixed Walker with a brown-eyed stare. "I heard some of this from Liam, but why don't you fill me in?"

Walker had learned, since he'd started liaising between Shifter Bureau and Shiftertown, how to stand toe-to-toe with Shifters, especially the alphas, and not let them intimidate him. He knew how to show he was on equal footing with Shifters but no threat to their homes, mates, or cubs. Shifters had grown to accept Walker, because they knew he didn't fake his respect or his understanding of their rules.

Walker faced Ronan now, relaxed, acknowledging that this was Ronan's territory but indicating he wouldn't jump into his pickup and flee the moment Ronan grew annoyed.

"The deal is that if Rebecca helps me on my mission of finding the missing Nancy Greene, the trespassing charges will be dismissed," Walker said. "But I have to spend my nights here while we're working on it, to keep an eye on her. I trust her not to go back out to the airport, but Shifter

Bureau doesn't. Me staying here keeps them off her back. Off yours too."

Ronan thought about this in his careful way, then he gave Walker a nod. "Makes sense."

Rebecca put one hand on her hip, as sexy in shapeless sweats as she'd been naked under the moonlight. "Yeah, I get it, but it still pisses me off."

"When big money is involved, the rules change," Walker said, trying not to think about the silver light touching her bare skin. "I'm sorry about that, Becks."

Rebecca let out a growl. "I know. I know. But I'm going to sulk for a while, all right? I'm also starving. Is there any food?"

The entire family guided Rebecca inside, Olaf holding her hand.

Cherie chattered excitedly. "Elizabeth made supper. Gobs and gobs of fried chicken. And macaroni and cheese. We had to keep Scott from digging in."

"Oh, right," Scott said. "I saw you wiping your greasy fingers after you walked past that platter of wings."

Their voices faded as they continued inside and the door banged closed, leaving Walker on the porch with Ronan.

"Thanks for what you did," Ronan said, his bear timbre rumbling the boards of the porch. "Rebecca's mad at you right now, but I know things could have been a lot worse." He let out a long breath. "It would have been hard on the cubs if anything had happened to her. Seriously hard. They've already been through too much grief. Thank you." Ronan extended his beefy hand.

Walker unslung his duffel bag to shake it. "I wasn't going to let them hurt her."

He'd have done anything to keep Rebecca safe—*had* done everything in his power to bring her home. The assholes at the pharmaceutical company had wanted Shifter Bureau to make an example of her. Walker had talked fast and pulled a lot of strings before they'd conceded to let Rebecca assist Walker on this mission—good PR if it succeeded. The pharma company execs could claim it was their idea.

Walker would have kept on talking until they let her go, no matter how long it took.

Ronan's gaze was shrewd, and his handshake firmed, threatening to crush. "Let's keep all this gushy stuff between you and me. Becks doesn't need to know—it would just piss her off more. And damn, can she be *crabby*."

Walker grinned as Ronan released his hand. "Done."

Ronan opened the front door, pulling the screen door closed behind him as he started in, shutting Walker out. "There's no extra bedrooms in the house, so you'll have to sleep in the Den." He pointed through the gloom at the dark bulk of the garage. "Stash your stuff in there and then come in for supper. My Elizabeth is getting to be a truly awesome cook."

———

Since Walker had been so helpful during all the trouble with Tiger, Ronan had welcomed him in Shiftertown. Rebecca watched from her end of the table as Ronan and Elizabeth spoke easily with Walker as supper progressed.

Rebecca was hungry—she shoveled pieces of chicken

and mac and cheese into her mouth as though she'd never get enough. She wanted to pick up the bowl of steaming vegetables and dump them down her throat, and she didn't even like veg. Bears needed a lot of food to keep them going on a good day, and tonight, Rebecca's adrenaline was high, her body still trying to throw off effects of the tranq.

But it was embarrassing. Walker was eating a lot—most men she knew did—but he didn't look as though ready to devour everything in sight. He managed to stay clean and neat as he went through what Elizabeth had dumped onto his plate, and then carefully spooned on seconds. Rebecca wanted to burp, but the sound would ring down the table. Not really the impression she wanted to give.

Though Walker had come often to Shiftertown in the past several months, he hadn't been to this house since the day he'd been brought here, unconscious and trussed up with duct tape, and left on the living room floor.

Rebecca had been assigned to watch over him. That had been fine, until he'd woken up, fought his way out of most of the tape, and tackled her trying to get away.

Wrestling Walker had been . . . interesting. He'd been holding back, she'd sensed, and she'd felt the steel strength of him as they'd scrabbled on the floor.

Walker had ended up half throwing Rebecca across the room. Then, instead of running away, he'd turned back, as though concerned he'd hurt her. Rebecca had been forced to go bear and tackle him.

Walker had never spoken of it. He didn't talk about it now, instead discussing Shifter happenings with Ronan.

The man had no business being so attractive. He was human, for crying out loud. But what a human. He'd traded his fatigues for civvies—jeans and a black T-shirt—clothes that clung to his body. Rebecca couldn't stop her gaze running over his wide shoulders, tight chest and abs under the T-shirt, and his strong arms, tanned and streaked with golden hair.

Rebecca didn't go for humans, right? Not for mating anyway. Rebecca was stronger than many human males, and she needed a Shifter who could take her.

She should go prowling tonight to relieve her itch—maybe that would help her cease thinking about rolling around the floor with Walker not ten feet from where they sat now.

But she couldn't go out and ease her frenzy, not with Walker here as her keeper. He'd hear her sneaking out and follow her.

Well, if he got an eyeful, so what? Would serve him right.

Rebecca stabbed her fork into her macaroni. Nah, she wasn't going to give him the satisfaction.

Besides, she didn't want to be with anyone else just now. There were great Shifters out there, but they didn't have Walker's square face brushed with blond whiskers, strong hands callused from years of serving in the military, a dark, rumbling voice that warmed her and made her skin prickle at the same time . . .

"So, Walker," Cherie was asking with her usual candor. "Do you have a girlfriend?"

Walker set down his fork, while Rebecca froze, her macaroni untouched. Walker wiped his mouth, then his fingers, every movement drawing her attention.

"Not right now," Walker answered without self-consciousness. "Why?"

"Oh, just curious." Cherie looked innocent, which didn't fool Rebecca.

Rebecca—and everyone else at the table—knew Cherie didn't ask on her own behalf. She wouldn't be interested in mating until she was through her Transition, which she wouldn't hit for another six or so years. Rebecca knew damn well why Cherie wanted to know.

"He's too old for you," Scott said to Cherie, playing along. He'd eaten more than anyone else, and his face had become a dark shade of red. "Too human for you."

"Yeah, well, I saw *you* looking at a human woman at Elizabeth's store yesterday," Cherie said, reaching for another chicken leg. "Looking, drooling, undressing her with your eyes."

Scott's flush deepened. "I don't drool. Anyway, how the hell do *you* know? You never stop talking long enough to notice what I do."

Cherie shrugged and nibbled daintily at her chicken.

Scott growled, a worrying sound. His hormones were flying around with his Transition, and Cherie wouldn't understand what that was like for some time yet. She only knew she could get her foster brother riled pretty fast these days.

Elizabeth rose hastily. "Can't forget dessert."

She ran out before Rebecca could offer to help and came back in with a simple and favorite after-dinner treat. Elizabeth had come to know her bear family well.

Walker leaned forward curiously as Elizabeth set a large bowl in the middle of the table, filled to the brim with plump, fresh blackberries.

"Yum!" Cherie's hands shot forward, her short feud with Scott forgotten.

In many Shifter houses, the dominant male got the food first, then he portioned it out to the others. In this house, however, Ronan had decreed, the cubs came first. Rebecca liked him for it.

Recently Scott had decided that all the adult females needed to be fed first, because it was important to keep them strong. He peeled the bowl from Cherie's grasp and shoved it at Rebecca.

Rebecca decided to humor him, forestalling Cherie's irritated growl with a look. Rebecca scooped berries out with a big spoon into the small bowls Elizabeth had provided. She gave one to Elizabeth and one to Cherie, then shoveled some out for Olaf and herself before sliding the bowl back to the middle of the table.

Scott gazed hungrily at the berries, ready to dive in, but he swallowed and passed the bowl to Walker, the guest.

Walker politely took a spoonful. Refusing offered food in a Shifter home was a grave offense.

Olaf dug into his berries with his fingers, his hands quickly becoming dark pink. Cherie, with the exuberance of youth, did the same.

"Bears love berries," Cherie said to Walker. "Thanks, Elizabeth. You went to a lot of trouble."

Elizabeth bounced Coby in her lap. "I didn't pick them myself. I bought them at Central Market. My whole job was washing them and putting them into a bowl. It's easy to make bears happy." She winked at Walker.

"I like blackberries," Olaf said around a mouthful. "But I wish we could have more fish."

"Yeah," Cherie said, smiling dreamily. "A big fat salmon."

Scott rolled his eyes. "Grizzlies."

"*I'm* not a grizzly," Olaf said, offended. "I'm a polar bear."

"You're a sweetie bear," Rebecca said. "And now a sticky one." She lifted her napkin, dipped it in her glass of water, and started wiping Olaf's mouth.

She caught Walker watching her with a guarded expression. In fact, mostly what he'd done since he'd sat down at the table was watch.

Scott finished off his bowl then dug into the serving bowl for the sad, smashed blackberries at the bottom. He ate those, licked his fingers, stretched, and let out a low growl.

His face was still flushed, his dark brown eyes shining. "I gotta go for a run." He shoved back his chair and climbed to his feet. "I'll help you clean up when I get back."

Scott was out the door before anyone could protest. Ronan rose, looking worried. "Becks, keep an eye on him. I would, but I have to get to work."

Rebecca was already going for her jogging shoes, which she kept beside the door. They were the ones she'd worn out to the airport last night—Ronan or someone must have fetched them home for her.

"Wait." Walker was next to her, his bulk between Rebecca and the front door, his scent like the night. "You can't go out there, remember?"

Rebecca put on a shoe while standing, hopping to keep her balance. "Scott could be running off anywhere. You want to keep Shifters out of trouble? You'll let me go after him."

Walker's face was hard—she had difficulty reading him,

but she saw indecision in his eyes. "Then I'm coming with you," he said, as Rebecca jammed on her other shoe. "He can't go to the old airport."

"Then we'll have to take him somewhere else."

Walker nodded. "I have an idea. I'll find him."

He was out the door as fast as Scott had moved. Rebecca snatched up her borrowed sweat jacket, pulled it on against the cool night air, and ran out after Walker.

CHAPTER FOUR

Scott had made it to the end of the street by the time Walker, in his truck, Rebecca again in the passenger seat, caught up to him. Scott had already shifted, and now Walker drove after a huge black bear running down the road at top speed.

Shifters out in their yards or on porches simply watched Scott go by. Cubs lifted their heads from playing to stare at him, but no one tried to stop him. Walker had seen this happen before—everyone in Shiftertown knew better than to get in Scott's way when he was trying to work off his Transition crazies.

Walker accelerated and pulled the pickup next to the galloping bear. "Scott!" Rebecca yelled through the window she'd opened. "Get in the back! We'll take you where you can run."

Scott turned, his eyes red as he snarled at her. He charged the truck.

Walker slammed on the brakes, throwing his arm around Rebecca and yanking her down. Scott hit the open window and spun off it, still snarling.

"You okay?" Walker asked as Rebecca fought her way upright.

"Yes, I'm fine." Rebecca glared with brown eyes that held both anger and concern. "What did you do that for?"

Walker returned his hands to the wheel, trying not to think about the feel of her soft body landing across his lap. "Because he was coming right at you."

Rebecca scowled, pushing her hair from her face. "He wasn't going to hurt me."

"How the hell can you know that?" Walker didn't keep the anger out of his voice. Scott was not in control when the Transition took over—why else would they bother with the chain in the wall?

Rebecca shook her head and didn't answer.

The truck listed as a large weight climbed into the back. Walker glanced into the rearview to see Scott shift back to human and wrap himself in the bundle of clothes Rebecca had left for him.

"He's good," Rebecca said. "Let's go."

Walker put his foot on the gas, and they left Shiftertown.

He drove out of Austin, heading east and south, way out past new development to emptier lands. Rebecca didn't speak, seeming uninterested in where they were going.

Walker took a series of dirt roads and ended up at the cement-floored arena that was the new place Shifters held their fight clubs. It was dark and deserted tonight; fight clubs followed a regular schedule. No one would come out here tonight.

Scott was out of the truck as soon as it slowed, throwing off the clothes. Naked, he ran into the darkness, and soon Walker heard bear growls.

He started to get out, but Rebecca shook her head. "He needs to run. He'll be back when he's ready."

Walker thought about the darkness, his tranq rifle tucked into the seat behind him, and what he'd learned about Shifters. He eased back into his seat and closed the door. He wasn't here to hinder Scott, and he'd seen Scott in Transition frenzy before. He ran, he felt better, he calmed down, and everyone went home.

Rebecca remained on her side of the truck, watching Walker with narrowed eyes. "How do you know about this place?"

Walker gestured with his rough fingers. A white scar ran across the backs of them, leftover from getting caught in a blast in the mountains of Afghanistan, where he'd been sent as part of a small A-team. "Dylan brought me out here."

"*Dylan* did?"

Dylan Morrissey, the former leader of Shiftertown and a force to be reckoned with, trusted no one. Walker watched Rebecca wrap her brain around the fact that Dylan had showed Walker the ultrasecret location of the ultrasecret fight club.

Dylan, however, had met with Walker often since Walker had taken over as liaison for Shifter Bureau. Dylan knew an asset when he saw one.

It had been Dylan's idea that Walker take up the task of looking for the missing human woman, Nancy Greene. The police hadn't done jack on the case since they'd figured out that Nancy was, in fact, a Shifter groupie. She'd become low priority then, but not to Dylan. A few phone calls and some conversations between Walker and his government contacts had gotten the case reassigned to Shifter Bureau, and now to Walker.

"Do you think if anyone else had brought me out here besides Dylan, that Shifter would still be walking around?" Walker asked.

Rebecca folded her arms and hunkered down in the seat, resting her knees against the dashboard. "Good point."

Heavy silence fell. Walker kept his hands on the wheel and searched the darkness, but he saw no sign of Scott.

Rebecca caught his concern and shook her head. "If I chase him, he'll go into fighting frenzy. Scott's not as tough as me, but he might forget who I am and try to hurt me. And then I'd have to take him down, and I might hurt *him*. He just needs to work off steam."

Walker listened, assessed. Made sense. "It's your call." He exhaled and made himself peel his hands from the steering wheel. "I need to bring you up to speed on the case."

She looked at him. "Joanne's sister has been missing for months—why are you only starting to look for her now?"

"*Officially* looking for her," Walker said. "Personally I started the investigation when Dylan told me about it this summer."

"Oh." She sounded a little less grudging.

"I got the case, since Shifters are involved," Walker said.

"And I keep telling you, Shifters are *not* involved."

"Maybe that's true, but they got pointed at, and no one will rest easy until it's proved beyond all doubt that Shifters didn't take her. That's where you come in."

Rebecca lifted her hands. "All right, all right. You're

stuck with me—I get it. I want to find this woman too. For her sake and Joanne's, not just to clear Shifters. Joanne dragged us into this, but she was scared. I don't blame her anymore." She straightened up in the seat, looking more interested. "So, what have you found out?"

Walker shrugged. "That no one knows anything. I interviewed Nancy's family and friends, coworkers, people at the coffeehouse she used to go to . . . Several times. I've gone over what she did on the last day anyone saw her, but she seems to have vanished. I'm not an investigator—I'm a soldier. I'm just doing what feels logical."

"I'm not an investigator either," Rebecca said. "But show me what you have, and we'll talk to Broderick. He's a pain in the ass, but for some reason, he's taken Joanne under his wing. He probably knows more about Nancy than anyone."

"I stashed my files in the Den. We can look them over and talk to Broderick tomorrow."

"He won't trust you," Rebecca warned. "Or me. We're not Lupines. Then again, he doesn't trust most Lupines either. He's hard to handle."

"I'm sure you can handle anyone, Becks."

He'd meant to make her laugh, but her voice went sharp. "Don't call me that."

Walker studied her. She was a woman of softness and curves, dark mystery around a core of steel. "I thought everyone called you that."

"They do. I mean, my family does." Rebecca moved restlessly, a woman not made to sit still. "It just sounds weird, coming from you."

Walker didn't bother answering, and silence fell again. He didn't know what next to say to her. He never did.

Hell, he didn't have a lot of experience with women, period, outside of bed. He'd had plenty of sexual encounters—no trouble finding volunteers—but relationships eluded him.

Getting sent all over the world into the most dangerous situations imaginable didn't make him want to form lasting ties. He had no intention of leaving a wife and kiddies bereft if something happened to him. And while many women had been attracted to Walker's dangerous side, they didn't necessarily want to settle down and pick out curtains with him.

Walker had learned to keep things casual, enjoy sex as a celebration, and remain alone. He'd made that choice a long time ago.

Then he'd met Rebecca. She was a tall, sexy-as-hell Shifter woman who turned into a bear—not your usual girl next door.

Though he'd fantasized about going to bed with her from the first day he'd met her, he'd never made the move to do it. Not because she could turn into a Kodiak and take him out with one paw if she wanted, but because she was different.

Rebecca was the first woman Walker had wanted to stick around with, to have conversations with—beyond this awkward one tonight—to be friends with. He'd once been close friends with a female lieutenant in his unit—it had never been sexual with her, but he'd been able to open up about things that he couldn't with his male friends. She'd married and left the army years ago, and he missed that kind of companionship.

A man talked to a woman about different things than he did with men—not that Walker talked much to other men either. Being commander of a tiny unit at Shifter Bureau

South meant he didn't have many peers at the office. Walker had to leave work to find companionship.

But it was tough to make lasting friendships with civilians when in the military, because the next thing you knew, you were yanked out of whatever town you were stationed in and transferred to another, in another state or maybe another country. You learned more about packing boxes than making friends.

Rebecca was different from his female lieutenant friend as well. Rebecca stirred Walker's most basic longings, the ones that wanted him to strip her clothes from her with slow hands and bury himself in her softness. He wanted to kiss every curve, wrap his mouth around the dusky areolas he'd seen twice now, and discover what she tasted like. He'd cup her neck and pull her to him for a long, burning kiss. Then he'd slide himself inside her and look into her eyes as they found the height of pleasure together.

He wanted that, but also to get to know her, and what the hell, pick out curtains with her. Walker knew damn all about choosing curtains, but she could teach him.

They were silent together, watching the night. Rebecca remained still, with the stillness only Shifters could have, but she had a presence that filled the truck's cab, warming Walker through. The October night was growing chilly, but Walker in shirtsleeves was fine. With Rebecca by his side, he'd never be cold.

Time passed. The moon moved across the sky. Clouds began to build on the horizon, swallowing the stars on the night's edge.

"Time we were getting back," Walker said when the digital clock on his dashboard clicked over to midnight.

Rebecca let out a breath as she unfolded herself and opened the door. "I'll call him in."

"With me," Walker said sternly.

Rebecca gave him an annoyed look, got out, and slammed the door.

CHAPTER FIVE

The night was crisp and, this far out of town, plenty dark. Refreshing. Austin had grown even since Walker had been stationed there, and the little towns between it and San Antonio had reached out to intertwine one another. In this area, ranchers and farmers still owned vast tracks of land, and the darkness was quiet, solid.

The metal rafters of the empty barn that housed the fight club creaked in the rising wind, wisps of dried grass skittering across the cement floor. Barrels that burned on fight club nights stood here and there, quiet and cold.

Walker had grabbed a lantern flashlight from behind his seat and also the tranq rifle, which he now loaded with a dose. Rebecca claimed she could bring Scott in with persuasion, but Walker recalled the way Scott had charged her and the truck and decided not to take the chance.

Rebecca eyed the tranq gun and gave him a frown, but both she and Ronan used tranqs on Scott when they didn't have a choice. Walker remembered his own frustrated teenage years—his mom, who'd raised him on her own, had probably sometimes wished *she'd* had a tranq rifle.

He and Rebecca walked without speaking to the end of the arena and gazed out into the rolling Texas grasslands, black under the night sky. The stars stretched overhead, blocked only by the clouds that were building with swiftness. No storm yet—if that one came in, it probably would hit in the early morning.

Rebecca stood on the edge of the concrete, cupped her hands around her mouth, and shouted, "Scott!"

The wind carried away the name, but Walker knew Scott would hear it. He turned on the flashlight and played it around, picking out grasses, a few bushes, a vast crop of weeds, and the remains of whatever the farmer had grown out here.

No bears in sight. Scott would be able to triangulate on the light though, as well as Rebecca's and Walker's scents.

Walker was about to move the light to another quarter, when eyes flashed in the darkness. A brief flare, then they were gone.

The creature the eyes belonged to was huge. And silent, disappearing with ease. Walker flashed the light around but didn't see it again.

He thought Rebecca would call out, coaxing Scott to come in. She didn't, only stood silently, the enticing curves of her covered with shapeless sweats.

Last night, the moonlight had touched her bare breasts, rendering her nipples points of darkness, with a deeper brush of darkness between her thighs. If Walker hadn't had a bunch of guys with rifles behind him, or assholes with shotguns running around in the dark, and the security team of the pharma company waiting for Walker to do something, the night would have ended a lot differently. Walker and Rebecca, on the ground, in the grass, to hell with tranq rifles and arrests.

Nope, he had to concede. Wouldn't have happened. Rebecca would have laid him out and then taken off. Walker wasn't that deluded.

The animal didn't reappear in his flashlight's beam. Walker turned, slicing his light another direction.

The next second, the flashlight was torn out of his hand, smacking to the concrete in a shattering of plastic.

Walker moved faster than thought, taking himself out of the way of the force that dove at him. Something large and warm barreled past, missing him by the barest inch. Walker spun in place, tranq rifle in hand, to face the fearsome bulk of a bear standing tall, eyes flashing red in the moonlight. Sparks from a Shifter Collar spun into the darkness.

This situation wasn't the same as when Walker had faced down Rebecca last night. She'd been angry, but Walker had come to know that Rebecca was nothing but careful. She knew how far she could go before she had to back off. Even in her rage, she had a core of control.

Scott was in his Transition, and all bets were off. The black bear snarled, then hit the floor on all fours, and charged.

Scott's Collar exploded into blue arcs, which didn't slow him down a second. Walker whipped himself aside again, but Scott had already learned his trick and compensated.

Several hundred pounds of bear came down on him. Walker had the tranq rifle half raised when it flew out of his hand, his arm going numb from the blow. Walker fell, rolling out of the way of the swiftly striking claws.

Another bear roared and hit Scott broadside. Walker rolled and came to his feet, grabbing the tranq rifle along the way.

A gigantic ball of fur, teeth, and claws rolled around the cement floor. The Kodiak and the black bear grappled and flailed, one ripping, fighting mass. Walker gripped the rifle, but the two were so entwined he couldn't be sure who he'd hit with the tranq. Walker supposed he could tranq both of them—if he could reload a dart fast enough. But then he'd have to haul *two* sleeping bears back to the pickup, and who knew what would happen if Scott woke up first.

Scott's Collar kept shocking, but Rebecca's never did. That meant Scott was enraged, needing to win, but Rebecca was only trying to get him under control, with no desire to hurt him.

She might have to anyway. They kept fighting, Scott's crazed fury giving him the strength to battle a Kodiak nearly twice his size.

Finally, Rebecca broke from Scott's hold. She brought up a massive paw, and before Scott could strike again, she smashed it down on the back of Scott's neck. She held Scott there, as he scrabbled to get out from under, like a mother cat with an unruly kitten. Except this kitten was a thousand pounds or so of muscle, the mother stronger still.

Rebecca's paw had foot-long, razor-sharp claws, but she never once broke Scott's skin. Walker aimed the tranq rifle again, but Rebecca growled and gave her massive head a shake.

The sparks of Scott's Collar started to fade. Scott struggled awhile longer, then the bear let out a little moan and went still.

Rebecca didn't let up her hold on him—maybe she'd seen this trick before. Minutes ticked by while she waited.

After about a quarter of an hour, Scott let out another moan, and he slowly, with a crackling of bone and cartilage, changed form.

A few minutes later, he was a panting, rawboned young man splayed out on his belly, moonlight brushing his skin.

"Oh, man," Scott said, his voice a croak. "Man."

Walker upended the tranq rifle. Rebecca shifted back to human, more smoothly than Scott had, but taking her time, as though not wanting to frighten him. Finally, the lush woman who invaded Walker's dreams emerged, her plump but strong arms gathering Scott to her.

"You all right?" she asked, stroking his hair.

Scott mumbled something into her neck. They sat that way, naked and holding each other, but there was nothing erotic about it. This was a mother and her cub, a protector and the protected, no matter what shape they happened to be.

Rebecca soothed and comforted, and Walker picked up the broken pieces of his flashlight, his world just a little bit changed.

———

"Hey, Becks," Scott said through the back window of the pickup.

They were heading toward the lights of Austin and Shiftertown, Rebecca once more in the sweats that smelled of human. She'd rip them off when she got home, toss them in the wash, and shove them at Walker in the morning.

She leaned back, exhausted from battling Scott, who'd given her a damn good fight, and then rocking him until he made it back to sanity.

Walker, the entire time, had backed her up without being told what to do. After she'd gotten Scott into a firm hold, Walker hadn't moved, hadn't said a word, while she'd waited to see whether Scott had been subdued or was just pretending to be.

No other human in her experience would have been as patient. Anyone else would have started babbling nervously, or gone ahead and popped Scott with the tranq. Walker had waited, as motionless as a predator, trusting Rebecca. It was a weird feeling, knowing he understood without explanation.

"What?" Rebecca asked Scott through the open window. Scott was sitting up, loose clothes on, looking no more dangerous than a young man who'd been out jogging.

"How do you know when your Transition is over?" he asked.

Walker glanced at him through the mirror then returned his gaze to the road, saying nothing. Again, he was trusting her to know how to handle the situation.

Rebecca thought about her answer, not sure what to say. Her Transition had been a long time ago, in the wild, and she'd had no Collar to battle.

"I don't know," she said. "You just do."

"Hmm." Scott was silent as traffic picked up, and the highway became a city street. "I think mine's over," he announced after a time.

"Might be," Rebecca said. "Wait and see."

"Yeah." Scott shrugged then stopped talking.

He did seem a lot calmer as they neared Shiftertown, his color returning to normal, his twitchiness gone. But the Transition could fool you—it was a roller coaster of hormones. Moving from cub to adult was an enormous change.

Rebecca had finished her Transition certain she'd waltz right out, find a great bear Shifter to hole up with, and have half a dozen cubs, easy as that. But bear Shifters had been few and far between up in the wilderness, and Rebecca had been shy around humans.

Now stuffed into a Shiftertown, she'd grown restless, wanting to find a mate but not sure how to. Didn't help that the few bears in this Shiftertown were in her clan, so she'd either have to go to another Texas Shiftertown—Shifters weren't allowed to leave their state without permission—or take a Lupine or Feline as mate.

Not appealing, though she'd gone out with Sean Morrissey, the Guardian, who was a Feline, for a time. But nothing had sparked, and both of them had known it. Rebecca liked Felines and Lupines as friends, but when it came to mating, that was different. Mating was for life.

But she had to do *something*. Or else she'd shove Scott out of the back of the truck, make Walker pull over, and jump his bones. She needed sex, needed it bad. Walker was male, tough, strong, and damn, could his eyes melt her in a heartbeat.

Rebecca clutched the seat until she felt its fabric tear. Fortunately, Walker soon pulled into Shiftertown and back to the large, busy house she called home.

Scott swung out of the pickup and leapt up onto the

porch without bothering with the steps. His energy was undimmed, and he started whistling.

Rebecca climbed out and started to follow him. Walker slammed the pickup's door behind her, startling her to a halt.

"We need to go over the files," he said.

Rebecca turned. "You mean *tonight?*"

"The sooner we start, the sooner I leave you alone. We go over the details now and begin questioning in the morning."

The last thing Rebecca wanted was to be holed up with Walker in the Den. Alone. Way too dangerous—for her.

"Sorry," she said, keeping her voice light. "I'm beat. See you in the morning."

Rebecca started for the porch. She sensed Walker behind her, unmoving, watching.

"It's not a request, Becks." He didn't raise his voice, didn't command, just said it.

Rebecca swung around. He remained by the truck, arms folded, the lights from the porch and the Den's door glistening in his buzzed blond hair and light blue eyes.

"I can't," she said swiftly. "I have to go out again."

Walker got around the pickup and in front of her with a rapidness that was almost Shifter. "Not without me, you don't."

Rebecca forced a smile. She and Walker were nearly the same height, his eyes looking straight into hers. "You won't want to go with me for this," she said, putting a coy note in her voice. "I built up a lot of adrenaline out there. I either have to run until I can't stay awake, or I find some company. Don't worry, I won't go anywhere near the airport. *Company* is more appealing tonight."

Walker returned her gaze calmly, his eyes not flickering

at her insinuation. Rebecca lifted her chin, daring him to comment, hoping he didn't realize she was shaking.

"I can't let you do either of those things," Walker said. "House arrest, Rebecca. You don't go out running without me, and you don't get to hook up with another Shifter for the night. Sorry."

He didn't sound one bit sorry, damn him.

"I don't think you understand." Rebecca transferred her hand to her hip. When she went into sultry mode, most guys, even Shifters, got nervous. "If you don't let me work off my craziness, there's no telling what I'll do to you in there." She glanced at the Den then back at Walker. "I'm a Shifter female. We're a lot of woman." She let herself smile again.

Walker looked Rebecca straight in the eye—not dropping his gaze to the V of her half-unzipped sweat jacket, not to the curve of her waist. He sucked her in with a stare that took no shit from anyone.

"I'll risk it," Walker said, then he turned his back and strode to the Den, not bothering to check whether she followed.

CHAPTER SIX

Rebecca wasn't the only one who needed to work off adrenaline. Walker's body hummed as he entered the Den, every nerve alert. He should say good night and lock himself in, but he knew damned well Rebecca would be out of there as soon as he shut the door. If she got caught outside Shiftertown without him, Walker might not be able to save her.

And he did not at all like her implication that she'd work off her stress with mindless, wild sex with a Shifter. Walker imagined that all she'd have to do would be go to Liam's bar, lean against the counter, and give the room a look. Every unmated Shifter male in the place would be fighting to land at her feet.

Not something he wanted to think about.

He waited at the door for her to enter. Moonlight and porch light fell on Rebecca's dark hair and glittered on the rage in her eyes.

If she took off right now, Walker would never catch her,

and they both knew it. He had to hope she understood that it was important at this moment to follow the rules.

Rebecca heaved a massive sigh. Walker tried not to watch her chest lift, but the loose sweat jacket couldn't hide her curves or the enticing way her unfettered breasts moved. She was wearing a T-shirt, but no bra. Every molecule in Walker's body knew that.

He moved away from the door as she charged toward it. If she pushed by him in a crush of scented female body, he'd throw regulations out the window. If the Bureau wanted her under house arrest, Walker would hole up with her, flush the key, and ride out the duration.

To keep things from exploding, he walked calmly to the table and laid out the files on Nancy Greene. The fridge held plenty of beer, and he took out two bottles, setting one down in front of Rebecca as she plopped into a chair.

"All right, what do we know?" she asked, as though they hadn't been silently fencing each other.

She scraped her hair from her face, twisted off the top of the beer bottle, and took a drink. A long one, her head going back, sweat on her throat matching the glistening condensation on the bottle. Beer commercials were full of sexy women with beer bottles, but none of them could outdo Rebecca.

"Walker?" Rebecca set the bottle on the table and peered at him, frowning.

She didn't know, did she? How hot she was? Walker couldn't afford to tell her. Rebecca would smile, and that would be the end of him.

He cleared his throat. "You already know that Nancy, Joanne's sister, is a Shifter groupie. She liked to frequent

Liam's bar as well as other Shifter bars from Austin to San Antonio. Addicted to Shifters, according to Joanne."

"Some humans are," Rebecca said as she studied the photos of Nancy. Her statement wasn't judgmental. Just a fact.

"Why are they?" Walker asked. "Is it the danger?"

Rebecca shrugged, which made the sweat jacket move again. "That, plus it's frowned upon by most humans—so the lure of something forbidden. And then, Shifter males are well-endowed and have the reputation of being good in the sack." She shot him a faint grin. "*They* think so, anyway. Most groupies are women, partly because there are far more unmated Shifter males than Shifter females."

"But not all groupies are women."

"Nope. Plenty of men will seek out the few Shifter females, or go for Shifter males—sometimes both. Shifters don't have the same taboos about sex as humans do, so the ones who like groupies oblige. You can get a pretty wild Shifter orgy going after some of the crazier Shifter bars close for the night."

Rebecca spoke impassively, but Walker couldn't help wondering whether she had participated in some of these orgies. He didn't want to picture her, naked and sweating, touching and being touched by human men and Shifter males, maybe by both at the same time.

The visions wouldn't stay out of his head. With her next to him, filling the space with her warmth and spice, the images multiplied. Rebecca arching back, her bare breast lifting toward a mouth—his mouth, he realized. The man with his hands all over Rebecca in Walker's daydream looked exactly like himself.

Shit. Walker desperately conjured thoughts of freezing rain, desert winds in winter, cold baths out of his army helmet in places with no hot water . . .

Shifters could scent changes in body temperature and pheromones. If Rebecca realized that Walker was growing needier by the second, this would fall apart fast. She wouldn't even have to scent it. Walker stood right next to her, and all she'd have to do was turn her head to see how hard he was.

"Poor kid," Rebecca said softly.

Walker jerked his attention back to the files. Rebecca held a photo of Nancy, one taken at a Shifter bar. Nancy's face was painted with cat whiskers, the tip of her nose black, and fake cat ears stuck out of her thick brown hair. She wore a skimpy, leopard-spotted dress that barely covered her. Nancy smiled broadly at the camera, a beer in her hand, a thick male arm draped around her neck.

"Looks like she's having a good time," Walker remarked.

"Too good. Shifters who like groupies just use them." Rebecca shook her head. "They won't take them as mates. That's what humans don't understand."

Walker frowned. "What exactly don't we understand? Explain it to me."

Rebecca flashed Walker a look he couldn't decipher. "Shifters are geared to mate and have cubs. That's what we're driven to do. Mating carries on our families, our clans, our species. So we like sex, and we don't stop ourselves."

"But sex doesn't necessarily mean mating for life," Walker said.

"No, it's just frenzy. Shifters understand this, and we don't worry too much about unmated Shifters having lots of sex. But what we really want—what we crave deep down inside ourselves—is the mate bond."

Walker took the chair beside her. "I've heard that, though no one has really explained it to me. It's like a soul-mate thing?"

"It's a little more complicated than that. It's a joining." Rebecca put her hand to her heart, between her ample breasts. "Like invisible tethers that run between the male and female Shifter, binding them together. But it doesn't necessarily always happen. Like I said, we're driven to pair up and have cubs. Mother Nature doesn't care if we form the bond, as long as we have the cubs. So two Shifters can go through the actual ceremony but never experience the true mate bond. That doesn't happen often anymore, but it's pretty sad when it does. Those Shifters have a family—cubs —but there's always something missing."

"Like humans marrying for money and then realizing they have an empty relationship."

"I guess. I don't know much about humans, but that sounds close." She looked puzzled. "Humans marry for money? Why?"

"I don't know. Survival. If you're human, you either have to work your ass off or find someone to take care of you. I never cared about money, so I never really thought about it."

Rebecca's frown eased away. "So what do you care about?"

Walker lined up the few photos of Nancy. "Doing my job well. Helping people as much as I can. Sleeping at night."

"With nothing on your conscience?"

"Something like that."

Rebecca lowered her head to her folded arms, looking up at him, her hair spilling around her face. "You slept well at night in war zones? Where people were killing other people?"

"I was a medic. I went deep behind the lines and got medical attention to those who'd never have had it otherwise."

Rebecca batted her eyelashes. "What a hero."

"Huh. And don't look virtuous and tell me Shifters are never violent. I've been to the fight club."

Rebecca's head came up, her eyes flashing. "We go to the fight club because we aren't allowed to run off our aggression." She jabbed at the black and silver Collar around her throat. "We have to wear *these*, and be confined to Shiftertowns, because humans are too stupid to understand Shifters. We fight, sure, but we don't make devices that kill massive amounts of people just to prove we can."

Walker lifted his hands. "How about we stop the conversation right there?"

"Right, stop it when I'm making a good point."

"Stop it, and go back to what we're supposed to be discussing. I agree about the Collars—humans put them on you because they're afraid of you. Shifters have a lot of honor. They also can be incredibly destructive, so don't pretend humans have the monopoly on violence."

Rebecca glared at him. "I thought we were finished with the conversation."

"We are. I just wanted to have the last word."

Walker hoped to make her laugh, but her brown eyes were filled with anger.

"I said 'poor kid' about Nancy because *humans* weren't

fulfilling her," Rebecca snapped. "She had to try to find happiness with Shifters."

"That's not what you meant." Walker touched the picture of Nancy smiling at them. "You meant she wouldn't find happiness with Shifters because they'd be looking for mates and the mate bond, but are happy to use her for plain old sex."

Her eyes flickered, and Walker knew he was right. "Shifters can form the mate bond with humans," Rebecca said, as though determined to argue with him, no matter what. "Look at Liam and Kim. Ronan and Elizabeth. Hell, Tiger and Carly. And Tiger's halfway to insane."

"A human woman is probably what Tiger needs then," Walker said. "Then again, sweet little Carly wrapped me in duct tape and let Tiger dump me into the trunk of her car."

Rebecca's angry look softened. "Yeah, I like Carly." A smile pulled at her mouth. "I noticed you slipped out of that duct tape without much problem. And then picked your way out of handcuffs. You don't stay down."

"Nope." Walker straightened the pictures again, trying not to remember again how Rebecca had stripped off all her clothes in her effort to *keep* him down.

Rebecca abruptly shoved the file away. "I can't do this."

"Sure you can. If we sift through the information long enough, it will lead us to something."

Her glare returned. "No, I mean, sit here with you. I was tranqued, locked up, threatened, put under house arrest, *and* had to chase after an unruly bear in his Transition. I don't like to be confined." She scraped back her chair and got to her feet. "Seriously, it makes me crazy."

"Claustrophobia?"

"Maybe a little." Rebecca rubbed her arms, shoulders coming up, body shuddering. "I grew up in wide-open spaces. Sticking a Kodiak bear in a city is pretty stupid."

She started pacing, and Walker observed her quietly. He thought he knew what she felt—sometimes in the field, especially in dangerous, dangerous places, the confinement to a compound or a hiding place behind the lines could make a guy stir-crazy.

He rested his arms on the table as he watched, as though relaxed, but he was ready to stop her rushing out the door if he had to.

"Spar?" he asked.

Rebecca halted, pivoting to look at him. "What?"

"Do you spar?" Walker asked. "To make yourself feel better?"

"Yeah." Rebecca looked puzzled. "Sometimes. With Ronan."

Walker stood, straightened the file, and walked to the door. "Come on, then," he said, and stepped outside into the cool night.

CHAPTER SEVEN

Rebecca blinked for a stunned few seconds, then she hurried after him.

Walker waited for her, his pale hair a smudge, his black T-shirt blending into the darkness. Inside the Den, lamplight had touched tanned arms, the muscles under his scarred skin beckoning her gaze. Walker was a fine specimen, no argument.

The wind was rising, but only a little, the storm hanging out on the horizon debating whether to strike. The wind ruffled Walker's T-shirt as he bent to unlace his boots and pull them off.

Rebecca studied the lithe lines of his back, the play of his shoulders and hips as he performed the simple task. He pulled off socks as well and straightened up, his brows rising as he found her standing next to him, gazing at him. Rebecca quickly toed off her sneakers, stepping barefoot into the grass.

Grass in Texas could be tricky, she'd learned her first

summer. Stickers and chiggers abounded to gorge on bare flesh. Ronan, however, made sure their lawn was trimmed back and planted over every fall, and now it was a soft pad of winter rye. The thin green spikes of grass poked up between Rebecca's toes, tickling them.

Walker stood relaxed, weight even on both feet. He gave her a nod—ready.

So he wanted to spar with a bear, did he? Rebecca didn't wait for him to set up a series of moves. She went for him.

He expertly caught her roundhouse kick, wrapped both hands around her ankle, and pushed her back. Rebecca hopped to regain her balance, wrenching her foot free of his grip. Walker didn't give her time to recover—he followed her with thrusts of fists she barely blocked.

Rebecca spun out of reach, then darted around him in a sudden move. She leapt at him, ready to thump both fists to his shoulders, then whirl away and finish up with a good kick to his kidneys.

Walker ducked, caught her, and used Rebecca's momentum to shove her harmlessly aside. She never touched him.

Rebecca halted and faced him, breathing hard. Damn, she must be getting soft. Sparring with Ronan and Scott should have made her more than a match for a human, even a combat-trained one. But either Ronan wasn't working her hard enough, or Walker was simply that good.

Walker didn't let her rest. He came for her, ducking when she took a defensive swing, and got under her reach. Rebecca found warm, virile muscle against her, a tall, hard body that wouldn't stop until it won.

Walker slid his foot behind hers, and before she could

jerk away, Rebecca was falling, the ground rushing up to her. She landed on her back, cushioned by his arms, his face an inch from hers.

His blue eyes glittered in the moonlight, a smile touching his mouth. "You're good," he said. "Too bad I was trained to fight people trying to silently kill me. You're just playing."

"Oh, yeah?" Rebecca started to roll, but he rolled with her, and she found herself flat on her back again, still pinned.

"If you were really trying to hurt me, your Collar would go off," Walker said, his voice rumbling against her chest. His hands were on her wrists, pushing them into the soft grass.

"We're sparring," Rebecca said, hearing the crack in her voice. "Working off steam."

Walker held her firmly but didn't crush her with his weight, exactly how he'd do it if they were in bed. Rebecca's breath came fast, and he must feel her pulse galloping under his fingers.

"If the fight club let females compete," he said, "you'd win."

Rebecca grinned, her fighting spirit returning. "Yeah, I'd kick Spike's ass."

"Could be—"

Walker's words cut off as Rebecca surged up, her legs clamped around his, and rolled them both over. Walker landed on his back with a grunt.

Rebecca planned to come to her feet and dance away, but her momentum was ripped away by Walker's strong grip, and she kept rolling. She landed on her back—*oof*—with Walker, tight and strong, on top of her once more.

His scent filled her, melting away every hurt she had. He smelled of warmth and the night, power and man. Rebecca's fingers closed on the back of his loose pants, but not to throw him off her. His warm, firm backside was smooth beneath the cloth, and she wanted to grab on and not let go.

She had to get away from him before she did something stupid. Rebecca struggled, but Walker held her firmly in place.

She took a gasping breath, pretending he scared her. As a male, Walker should immediately release her, declare he hadn't meant to hurt her, help her to her feet, apologize.

Walker's smile broadened. "Sweetheart, I've fought women who tried to play frightened rabbit so they could reach for the nearest hand grenade. Or put a garrote around my neck."

Rebecca stilled, aghast. "Seriously?"

"Women make good assassins. Most men underestimate them."

"But not you," Rebecca said.

His grin went wicked. "Nope."

"You're not a gentleman then."

"Not when I'm fighting for my life, no."

Rebecca, who'd gone limp while he'd held her, smiled back at him. "All right. If you want to play dirty . . ."

She relaxed and let the Kodiak bear in her come. Her hands changed to giant paws with long claws—she moved them so the claws wouldn't rip straight into Walker's skin. Her body changed and grew, splitting the sweats she wore.

Rebecca was good at shifting—she could control which parts of her changed first. Many Shifters couldn't; they simply had to let nature take over. But Rebecca's face could remain human, while her limbs took on the strength and agility of a bear's.

Walker made an *unh* sound as Rebecca flipped him easily onto his back, her bear paws landing on his shoulders. Walker struggled with all his strength, but no man could out-wrestle a Kodiak, unless the Kodiak let him.

Rebecca scrambled off him and sprang to her feet, letting her bear come all the way. She rose to her full height, growling and rumbling under her breath. No sparks lit her Collar, because she had no wish to kill Walker. Just scare him a little.

Walker jumped to his feet in a sinuous move, the guy in great fighting shape. He stood with hands on hips, an amused expression on his face. "You're right, that's playing dirty."

Rebecca growled again, lifting her muzzle, and then she shifted back to human, letting her bear flow down until she stood once more on human feet. The sweats were in shreds on the grass, starlight and the remote storm's breeze touching her skin.

"I play to win," Rebecca told him.

"I see that." Walker's gaze took in her entire body. He didn't shuffle and get embarrassed; he blatantly stared. "Guess what, Becks." His voice went soft. "I play to win too."

He came at her in a blur of motion. Rebecca scrambled back, fending off kicks from his bare feet, blows from his fists, his body never in one space for more than a second.

Rebecca ended up pushed against the corner between porch and house, deep in shadow. Walker's warmth embraced her, the cloth of his T-shirt soft on her breasts.

His face was an inch from hers, his breath on her skin. His eyes glinted in the dim light, his hand pressed to the wall next to her head.

I play to win too. The words echoed in her head.

Walker had said men underestimated female assassins, but Rebecca had underestimated him. She'd decided to tease him, to teach him a lesson, and here she was, standing against him, stark naked, while he simply looked at her and held all the cards.

Rebecca closed her hands into fists, trying to still her rapid heartbeat. She could kiss him, take the mouth that was hovering so near hers. Surrender.

It wouldn't be much of a surrender. More like relief.

Walker did nothing. He didn't try to kiss her, touch her, take her down, gloat. He only looked at her, his gaze tangling with hers, his scent warm and embracing in the cool darkness.

They stood still, breath mingling, his body warming her. Inside the house, the television went on, Olaf watching his favorite shows, most of which he still didn't understand. Cherie yelled something at Scott, and Scott said, "Yeah, yeah." Coby gurgled, and Elizabeth answered in a sweet peal of laughter.

Outside, Walker and Rebecca were perfectly silent, perfectly still, while the night went on around them.

Walker's gaze swept over her again, then he abruptly pushed himself from the wall.

"Get some sleep, Becks," he said, as cool as if they were standing in the middle of a coffeehouse, not Rebecca naked and against him in the yard. "We'll start on the case in the morning."

He walked away. Just like that. Cornered her, made her shake with need, then left her.

"Walker." She went after him.

He turned. "What?"

Rebecca reached him. She couldn't leave it like this. Not as though fire hadn't slammed through her, not as though she hadn't been craving him since he'd pointed the tranq gun at her last night.

But she stood tongue-tied, not knowing what to say. Rebecca, who could confound any male with her teasing and innuendo, couldn't think of a single word.

She reached out and ran a finger across his cheek. Rough whiskers brushed her fingertip.

A muscle moved in Walker's jaw, his eyes flickering. She saw a flash of heat, like lightning in dry grasslands, then he dampened it—swiftly, deliberately.

Rebecca lowered her hand. "Good night," she said softly.

Walker swallowed. He studied her again, eyes filling with more fire. He didn't try to touch her or kiss her, but he didn't run away either.

"Good night," he said, his voice blending with the night.

He didn't move, waiting for her to turn away first. Rebecca drew a breath, stepped back, scooped up the torn sweats from the grass, and hurried to the porch. Holding the clothes in front of her to cover herself under the porch light, she looked back down to him, ready to say good night again.

Walker was gone. Nothing in the yard betrayed he'd ever been there, except for the gleam of his pickup in the drive-way, and the lingering sound of a door slamming as he vanished back into the Den.

———

BRODERICK LIVED IN THE MIDDLE OF SHIFTERTOWN IN A two-story bungalow with a spreading yard shadowed by tall, thick trees. A lanky Shifter lounged on the porch steps, an adult, but one not much past cub age, maybe a year older than Scott.

The Shifter climbed rapidly to his feet when he saw Walker approaching, Rebecca at his side.

"Brod!" he yelled. "It's the she-bear and that guy from Shifter Bureau."

Walker stopped at the edge of the grass, knowing from experience that walking into a Shifter's yard without his permission was a good way to get attacked. Most Shifters wouldn't dream of attacking a man attached to the bureau, but Walker liked to show respect. Plus, Broderick was one of the few who'd not worry about confronting him.

Broderick, a wolf Shifter in a muscle shirt that showed off his tatts and knotted shoulders, stepped out onto the porch.

Rebecca pushed past Walker and strode toward the house. The brush of her body, the scent of her hair, brought too vividly the memory of leaning against her in the dark, the house solid behind her. He'd felt every curve of her, the press of her chest with every breath.

Their faces had been an inch apart, Rebecca's hot brown gaze holding his, then sliding to his lips. His heart had thudded, blood hot. The urge to take her mouth, to mold her body with his hands, to sink into her softness, had undone him.

He'd made himself tear away from her and walk back into the Den, his cock hard and straining, his body aching. The sparring was supposed to have worked off their steam—

instead, it had ramped it up. Even a brutally cold shower in the Den's bathroom hadn't helped.

The storm had hit as he'd stood under the freezing water, wind shaking the Den, rain pounding. Then it was over, the storm dispersing as quickly as it had come. His encounter with Rebecca had felt like that—a pulsing maelstrom, over before he'd realized it had begun.

This morning, when Elizabeth had invited him inside for breakfast, Rebecca had barely spoken to him. She'd said, "Oh, hey, Walker," while chewing a slice of toast, then ducked into the kitchen and hadn't emerged until Walker had been ready to leave.

Now Rebecca walked toward the house without hesitation. "Broderick, we—"

Broderick was off the porch and in front of her in one rapid move. He was taller than Rebecca by half a head, and though Rebecca was no weak, petite woman, Broderick was a male Shifter enraged.

Screw this. Walker left the invisible *do not cross* line and headed for them.

"Don't you understand territory, Becks?" Broderick was rumbling in his broken-gravel voice. "This is *mine*. Yours is over there." He lifted an arm, tight with muscle, to point down the street toward Ronan's house.

"Don't give me territory crap," Rebecca said, unworried. "I'm an unmated female, and he's human. We can't take your territory even if we wanted to. Shifter law."

Broderick's gray eyes narrowed. "Have you noticed that we don't live in the wild anymore? If humans want our territory, they'll just take it."

"Not today," Walker said. Broderick's hot alpha stare

came to rest on him, but Walker had trained himself not to flinch. The Taser holstered on his belt helped with his confidence.

"So, tomorrow, then?" Broderick's voice bore a sharp growl.

Rebecca broke in. "Can you two calm the testosterone and listen for a sec?" She put her hands on her hips. Broderick reluctantly dragged his gaze from Walker and returned it to Rebecca. "We came to talk to you about Joanne and her sister."

Another low growl, one that had Broderick's eyes turning from intense gray to Shifter white. "Why didn't you say so?" Broderick flashed his warning look over Walker again before he shrugged. "Come in. Wipe your feet. Aunt Cora just did the floors, and she's one mean wolf if you get them dirty."

CHAPTER EIGHT

Walker always found it interesting to walk into a Shifter's house for the first time. Interesting in an *I could be killed if I look at something the wrong way* kind of deal.

Broderick McNaughton and his family were in a pack now led by a female called Glory, who'd taken over when the last pack leader had been killed. The Lupines in Broderick's pack had been leery of having a female lead them at first, but they were taking to it. Glory wasn't just any female, however —she was a force of nature, and her mate was Dylan Morrissey. Whoever messed with Glory messed with Dylan, and even Broderick was content to let things remain status quo.

Broderick lived in this house with his aunt and three younger brothers. They took up the whole bungalow, four big males squeezing in with one female who somehow kept them all in line. The family was powerful, high in their clan. If Glory or any of her future offspring fell, Broderick would be pack leader, and he knew it.

Broderick seemed to fill the space around him, dominating the house. He didn't have to posture much—he stood easily in his jeans and sleeveless shirt, and everyone knew he was in charge.

He didn't invite them to sit down, though Aunt Cora brought out some iced tea in cold glasses.

"You two must be thirsty," she said to Rebecca and Walker. She was on the small side for a Shifter, gray haired and tiny compared to her nephews. "You drink that while Broderick looks up the word *hospitality.*"

Broderick rolled his eyes but said nothing. Walker sipped the tea politely, knowing it meant a breakthrough. Aunt Cora would never have offered if Broderick hadn't okayed it. This was his way of indicating he was willing to talk.

"You speak a lot with Joanne?" Walker asked, ice clinking in his glass.

"Yeah, I do." Broderick straightened, his brows drawing together. "What about it?"

Rebecca laughed, the throaty sound conjuring up the fantasies Walker had had in the shower last night. Even the freezing water hadn't been able to shut them out.

"Don't broadcast any harder," Rebecca said to Broderick. "You like her."

"I feel sorry for the kid," Broderick rumbled. "She's worried about Nancy, and no one has done a damn thing to help her."

"The police have investigated," Walker pointed out, though he privately agreed they hadn't done much.

"Huh." Broderick's scowl deepened. "The minute they figured out that Nancy was a Shifter groupie, they backed off. They pretty much said it was her own fault she got snatched."

"I don't know," Rebecca said. "I remember the cops searching through Shiftertown fairly thoroughly for a while. Joanne had them convinced a Shifter had stashed her sister somewhere. Remember?"

"Yes, I remember," Broderick conceded. "They were pains in our asses. Didn't help find Nancy, though, did it? They were looking in the wrong place. Then they just gave up."

"I plan on looking in the right place," Walker said. "Which is where you come in. What has Joanne told you? I'd like to talk to her as well."

Broderick's belligerence returned. He stepped to Walker, towering over him, but Walker had learned a long time ago that height really didn't have anything to do with strength of will or ability to win a fight. He currently saw four different ways he could take down Broderick before Broderick could do much damage. Walker wouldn't even have to spill his tea.

"Leave Joanne alone," Broderick snarled at him. "She's been through enough."

"Easy," Rebecca said, becoming a solid wall at Walker's side. "We only want to find her sister. No one's touching Joanne."

"Believe it or not, I'm trying to help," Walker said. "It's my job."

Broderick didn't look appeased, but on the other hand, he didn't go for Walker's throat.

"If you can help fill in the gaps," Walker went on, "maybe we can all figure this thing out together."

The community appeal didn't soften him, but Aunt Cora looked up at her nephew and said, "Do it for Joanne, Brod. I like her."

Broderick wasn't the type to admit defeat, but he gave Walker a grudging nod. "Joanne and I already looked," he said. "Nancy is a true groupie. Dresses up, goes to Shifter bars. Made it her goal to not go home until she had a little Shifter sex. She went to every Shifter bar in Austin, and then spread out across Hill Country and down into San Antonio. She had friends she'd take road trips with, going to Shifter bars across South Texas. She was obsessed."

Broderick's disapproval radiated from him. From what Walker had observed, Broderick wouldn't turn down a willing groupie, but he clearly didn't like them. As Rebecca had said last night, many Shifters simply used groupies for easy sex.

"Then we check the Shifter bars across South Texas," Walker said.

"You think Joanne and I haven't?" Broderick asked, but his hostility had eased a little. "We talked to her friends, went to the bars, talked to the Shifters there. Not that they were interested in telling me much."

Not surprising. If Broderick had swaggered in as he usually did, expecting to take charge, he'd likely ended up in more fights than conversations.

"No kidding," Rebecca said, echoing Walker's thoughts. "Did you find out anything at all?"

"Sure, we did. Nancy was popular, but the Shifters she was regular with hadn't seen her in a while. Even in her favorite bar, she hasn't been around much."

"Which is her favorite bar?" Walker asked. That was the

place to start—where Nancy was the best known. Broderick might have gotten stonewalled when he threw his weight around—diplomatic questions could work better.

"Place called Shooters. Out east of San Antonio. I went there twice, took Joanne the second time, to see if she recognized anyone. Nothing."

Walker might find the same nothing, but it was a place to start. "Thanks," he said sincerely.

"If you're going out there, I'm coming with you," Broderick said. "So is Joanne."

Rebecca put her hands on her hips. She was wearing a black T-shirt this morning with a V neckline that clung to every curve.

"Oh, right," she said. "What's your idea of questioning? Slamming a Shifter up against a wall and banging his head until he answers? Walker and I were going to try something a little more subtle."

"Like what? Turning into a giant bear?" Broderick demanded. "Lots of Lupines down there. If you knock them out with bear smell, they won't be able to answer you."

"Lupines think they have such great senses of humor," Rebecca said, shaking her head. "I just have to smile at them, shithead. And Walker has his Taser. We'll get answers."

Broderick's eyes narrowed. "So *you'll* take off your shirt, and Shifter Bureau here will Taser them while they stare at your breasts? Real subtle, Becks."

Walker lost his patience. "I'm about to go for the Taser right now," he said sternly. "Broderick, I'll welcome your help as backup—Joanne will know Nancy's friends and conquests better than I or Rebecca. But as *backup*—right? A little covert ops will help us more than you smacking people around and Rebecca flashing them." Not that the last thought didn't make Walker tighten. "Call Joanne. Set it up for tonight."

Both Rebecca and Broderick looked at him in surprise, and so did Aunt Cora, clearly not used to humans giving orders.

Too bad. Walker had a job to do, and arguing about who was in charge only slowed things down. He'd learned that a long time ago. In his line of work, people argued, people died.

Aunt Cora was the first to respond. "Sounds like a good plan. I'll call Joanne, if you're going to stand around playing who's alpha Shifter all day." She turned and headed for the landline phone that rested on a table near the stairs.

Broderick heaved a sigh. "I'll do it, Aunt . . . Leave it, all right? Damn it." He broke away from Rebecca and Walker, striding to his aunt, closing his hand around the receiver the same time she did. "I *said*, I'd call her."

Rebecca grinned, dark eyes sparkling. "Let us know, all right?" She set down her mostly empty glass of iced tea and started for the front door.

Did she have to saunter like that everywhere? Hips swaying, jeans clinging to her sweet ass?

Walker dumped the rest of the iced tea down his throat, hoping the cold of it would dampen his fire. He needed to hurry and find Nancy Greene and get out of Shiftertown before he died of combustion.

———

Back at the house, Walker outlined his plans. He sat at the dining room table, near the ring in the wall Ronan had once cuffed him to, and spread out his notes.

Walker chained to the wall had been as calm and confident as Walker sitting here today. He'd known then that he'd eventually get away, just as he knew now that he was in charge. The man's confidence filled the room.

Every other person from Shifter Bureau that Rebecca and Ronan had dealt with had been nervous, and overcompensated with pushiness and obstruction. They'd had to face many of these assholes as they'd worked to bring the foster cubs to Austin. No one had wanted the care of Scott, Cherie, and Olaf, but Shifter Bureau had made Ronan jump through many hoops to get them officially accepted into this Shiftertown and allowed to live in his house.

Walker was nothing like those bureaucrats, maybe because he was on the military attachment side, and he'd been assigned to the bureau, not there by choice. Whatever the reason, Walker was calmly competent, taking charge without being obvious about it.

Rebecca had hoped they'd discuss their plans together, alone, in the Den. She'd been a mess inside since he'd pressed her against the wall last night in the dark, his lips a breath from hers. His body had been firm, no softness. She'd wanted to run her hands over every plane of him, lick his mouth, then take his hand and lay it over her breast.

She'd wanted it so much she'd lain awake all night thinking about the encounter and how it might have gone differently. Walker could have let Rebecca open his jeans, he might have hooked her knee over his arm, raising her leg so he could thrust up into her. It would have been quick and hot, dirty sex over too soon. But she'd have savored it the same as if it had lasted for hours.

Rebecca swallowed and tried to keep from breaking into a sweat. Fortunately, everyone in the room was fascinated with Walker, and not looking at Rebecca.

Another reason to talk to him alone—besides her hormones—was that the whole family decided they had to get in on the discussion. Elizabeth was off running her store in SoCo, but Ronan was home. He held his cub in his giant arms, while the three foster cubs and Elizabeth's younger sister, Mabel, gathered around and "helped."

"If you're going covert," Mabel, whose hair was fuchsia this month, said, "you can't march inside a Shifter bar and start questioning people, like Broderick did. You have to blend in." Her smile widened. "You have to go as a groupie."

"Don't look at me," Rebecca said, hands raised. "I can't pass for a groupie, no matter how much makeup I put on. Shifters will be freaked out as soon as they scent me coming, as it is."

"Then you shouldn't go at all," Ronan said, his bear growl filling the room.

"Yes, I should," Rebecca said quickly. "You think Walker can infiltrate a Shifter bar without Shifter backup? They'll eat him alive."

"She's not wrong," Mabel said, her eyes narrowing as she scanned some of Walker's notes. "I know that bar, Shooters. Humans who aren't groupies don't go there. It's Shifter dominated, if you know what I mean. In fact, I should probably go with you. I know how to do the whole groupie thing."

Walker, Ronan, and Rebecca answered at the same time. "No!"

Mabel looked annoyed. "I'm a grown woman. I can go where I want to."

Ronan answered before the other two could. "You're the sister of my mate, and if you go, she'll *kill* me. You're staying out of this one."

Mabel's frown deepened, but it said a lot about how much Mabel had calmed down since Ronan and Elizabeth's mating that she subsided and didn't argue.

"She is right though," Walker said once everyone was quiet. "We do need an excuse to wander around the bar asking questions. If groupies are the only humans who go in, a groupie will go in."

"Joanne," Rebecca said. "She knows how to make up like one. She passed for a groupie for a long time before any of us caught on."

Walker was shaking his head, his eyes sparkling with humor. "Not Joanne. I don't want to risk her. I was talking about me."

Rebecca's eyes widened. "You?"

"Yep." Walker grinned at her shock. "Dress me up, and I'll go in as your date."

CHAPTER NINE

Everyone but Rebecca embraced the idea. Mabel and Cherie—the two were nearly the same age—excitedly brought down Mabel's makeup kit, and they started transforming Walker while the others watched.

Rebecca sat on the other side of the table, not sure what she was feeling as the rest of the family surrounded Walker and gave advice.

"More whiskers," Ronan said. "There you go."

"His eyes aren't right," Scott put in. "You want him a Feline groupie? Or a bear?"

"No one goes as bear groupies," Mabel said with a scoff. "It's Feline or Lupine."

"Why not?" Olaf asked. He stood at the edge of the table, small hands on the wooden surface as he looked up through the sea of adults working on a very patient Walker. "Don't people like bears?"

"I don't know, sweetie," Mabel said. "The groupies I

know do Feline and Lupine, and mostly Feline. Maybe it's easiest to find cat ears? Our store sells a lot of them."

"I think this is a bad idea," Rebecca said.

No one paid her any attention, except Walker, who gently moved Mabel's hand aside to look at her. "I don't. I can't go in as an ex-special forces, military attachment to Shifter Bureau. They might figure it out sooner or later, but we'll learn a lot before they do, if they think I'm a harmless idiot."

Harmless? Half of Walker's face was painted, his left eye outlined in black—Mabel had drawn eyeliner to a point on his temple, giving him an ancient Egyptian look. His eyelid was shaded in dark grays, his light blue iris standing out like a diamond in shadow.

The tip of his nose was black, a cat-like upside-down triangle. Mabel had spread a pale foundation over his face, softening the roughness of it, before she'd started drawing in the whiskers. She'd gone over his lips with black lipstick.

Mabel was skilled, and Walker didn't look harmless. He looked sexy, a man out shopping for a Shifter to be with.

With the other half of his face not made up, Rebecca could see what he'd look like once he'd found his lady for the night. His makeup would smear as he kissed her, the paint getting all over her face. They'd be standing up against a wall, or down on a bed, while they put hands and mouths all over each other.

Clothes off, lips meeting, bodies coming together in the dark.

Becks, he'd whisper as he touched her. *Rebecca . . .*

"Rebecca." Walker's voice was sharp. "Did you hear me?"

She jumped. "What?"

Walker's eyes narrowed as though he wondered what was wrong with her. "I said, I'll put up with it for the sake of getting intel. I'm used to it."

"Really?" Mabel asked, interested. "You've done this before?"

"Not *this*." Walker waved his hand at his face. "But other things."

"Ooo, tell us."

Walker sent Mabel a wise look. "Can't. National security. Need to know, only."

"Oh. Right."

Mabel's eager grin vanished, and she tried to look as sage as Walker. Walker gave Rebecca the barest wink.

Her blood boiled, her skin prickling with heat. Rebecca stood up hastily, nearly knocking over her chair in the process. "I need to get some air."

The others stared at her in surprise. Rebecca straightened the chair she'd knocked askew and ran for the door, out into the October sunshine and cool air.

———

MABEL WASHED THE MAKEUP OFF WALKER'S FACE ONCE she had the design down and had taken a photograph for reference. She was good at this, Walker realized. Mabel, in her early twenties, had a brisk businesslike way about her, but also a sense of fun that Walker missed in himself.

He'd never thought, at her age, that he'd end up behind a desk at Shifter Bureau, trying to keep the peace between humans and Shiftertown. His military career was pretty much over, any thought of family gone, and he was about to spend Saturday night pretending to be a groupie in a Shifter bar.

But this was his job. He'd gone behind the lines to retrieve those in trouble before, and this was no different. A young woman was missing. Walker was good at getting people home safely, and he would do it now.

He'd hoped he could spend time sitting with Rebecca, going over the case files together, but by the time Mabel had finished with him, Rebecca, who he'd made sure hadn't gone farther than the front yard, had returned to the house and retreated to her bedroom. She'd taken the case file with her, so she wasn't refusing to help, but she didn't come out until time for supper.

Rebecca now hid in the kitchen with Elizabeth, helping prepare dinner for the crowd. The two women, assisted by Scott, carried out the feast, which the younger bears and Mabel made vanish.

Conversation was lively, and Walker warmed to it. He liked the openness of this family, most of them not related to each other, except by friendship and caring. He didn't have this in his solitary life. He focused on his missions, moved from place to place, and went home alone every night.

After dinner, they cleared the table, Mabel brought out her makeup kit again, and sat Walker down for his final costuming. Elizabeth helped her, the two women and the cubs closing around Walker.

He couldn't see Rebecca in the crush, but he couldn't have spoken to her even if he'd tried. Mabel had Walker half pinned to the chair, her round face next to his as she concentrated on drawing his eye markings with a steady hand.

Walker had once been captured on a mission, restrained, and tortured. Being pressed back into a chair while someone stuck something pointy near his eye still made him squirrelly. But he tamped down his instinctive reaction. He wouldn't hurt Mabel for the world.

"There." Mabel stepped back. "What do you think, Rebecca?"

Rebecca was at his side. She leaned down, her ample bosom in the tight black top she'd put on right next to his cheek. *Damn.*

"More here." Rebecca touched Walker's eyebrow. "He needs to look like he sits around thinking about sex with Shifters all day."

Mabel grinned, white teeth flashing, and touched her pencil to his face. Rebecca watched, then nodded. "You got it."

"Want to see?" Mabel asked Walker as she slid the cap onto the pencil.

"Doesn't matter," Walker said. He fought the urge to rub his face and started to rise, but Rebecca pushed him down with a firm hand.

"Ears," she said.

Elizabeth had brought them from her store. These ears, affixed to a headband, were white and furry with leopard spots on the outside, black fur on the inside. Rebecca took them from Elizabeth, leaned down, and fixed them on Walker's head. The plastic band was tight, but Walker didn't adjust it.

Rebecca regarded him critically, but Mabel grinned. "Love it. Picture!" Before Walker could stop her, Mabel had whipped out her cell phone and clicked it. "Oh, please say I can post this."

Rebecca peered at the phone, then the seriousness she'd worn all day vanished, replaced by a breathtaking smile. "That's a keeper. I say we have Elizabeth blow it up to poster size and hang it on the wall."

Rebecca laughed with Mabel, and Walker sat there and let them. When Rebecca laughed, the world was a good place.

"Maybe later," Walker told Mabel. "Keep it to yourself for now. Covert, remember?"

"Right." Mabel gave him another smile and tucked her phone away. "Go catch bad guys."

"You mean go question Shifters," Walker said, standing up. He took the ears off and set them on the table. "What's the best thing to wear?" he asked Mabel. "If I want to blend in with the other groupies, I mean?"

Rebecca folded her arms and looked him up and down. "Hot pants."

Mabel went off into a peal of laughter, and the Shifter cubs snickered.

Cherie volunteered the next idea. "I've seen the male groupies wear just jeans. Riding low. A loose button-down shirt—they have to wear a shirt to be allowed into the bar, but they can unbutton it while they're dancing."

Ronan's growl filled the room. "And when are you looking that hard at Shifter groupies?"

Cherie blinked in surprise. "I see them in Liam's bar all the time. So do you."

Ronan kept growling. "Yeah, well, I think I'll escort them out a little more often."

"She's not wrong," Scott put in. "They pretty much try to show off all they have. So do the women."

"Jeans, button-down shirt," Walker said. "Got it. I'll change, and we'll go."

"No underwear," Rebecca said, sending him a sly smile.

Walker's skin heated. He hid his sudden flush by snatching up the fake ears. "I'll think about it."

"Wait," Mabel said. "Elizabeth brought a tail too." She held it up, long and spotted—and very furry.

Walker studied the entire family full of grinning faces. They were making so much fun of him, and loving it.

"Overkill," Walker said. "I'm not walking around all night with that thing strapped to my ass."

Mabel slid her phone out again. "Just for a picture?"

"No," he said firmly but not unkindly, walked out the door, and shut it behind him.

———

REBECCA LEANED ON HER MOTORCYCLE, SHIVERING IN wind that had turned cool. Last night's storm was long gone, but it had left a lingering chill. She zipped up her leather jacket and thrust her hands into the pockets, knowing her sudden coldness came from more than the weather.

The light went off in the Den, and Walker emerged. In the glow of the Den's porch light, Walker did look very much like a Shifter groupie. Made-up face, tight dark jeans, leather jacket over loose shirt, the fake ears clutched in one hand, a small duffel bag in the other.

"Let's go," he said, heading for his truck.

Rebecca intercepted him. "If you truly were my groupie, you'd have me drive. We go on my bike."

She thought he'd argue, or toss her the keys to his truck and tell her they were taking that instead, but Walker shrugged, tucked the ears inside his jacket, and headed for the motorcycle. He stashed his duffel in the saddlebag, waited for Rebecca to mount, then swung himself on behind. He knew how to do it, no hesitation.

Rebecca was the one shaking as she pressed the starter. Ronan loved the old kick-starter on his motorcycle, but Rebecca liked electronic starters, faster when she was in a hurry, which was most of the time.

Because Rebecca wasn't a petite woman, her bike wasn't either. She had a large Softail, big enough for her frame, with a passenger seat behind her. She was used to extra weight when she rode, since she ferried Cherie and Scott all over the place. She balanced easily as she slid the bike along the driveway and out into the street.

What she was not used to was the warm strength of Walker, wrapping his arms around her to hold on. He knew how to do that too, steadying himself without impeding her. He'd been made to ride with her, she thought, the two becoming one as the bike rolled out of Shiftertown.

Rebecca tried to shut out the sensation of his hard body against her back, his weight perfectly in tune with hers. She leaned into the turn as she glided onto Airport Boulevard, and Walker kept balance with her.

Too bad they weren't heading out for a day of biking pleasure, the open road, taking their time, going wherever they wanted. She could ride behind sometimes, clinging to Walker's firm body while he took them into the wind.

They'd stop for the night in some roadside motel, tired, contented, and sleep spooned together in a thin-mattressed bed—after hours of kick-ass lovemaking, of course. More of the same the next day.

They could do it—this daydream didn't have to remain a dream. Shifters weren't allowed to travel between states, but Texas was huge. A biker could ride its roads for years and never see all there was to see.

Shooters lay to the east of San Antonio, on a highway that wound eventually to Houston. It was a roadhouse, lying by itself outside the nearest small town, surrounded by a lighted dirt parking lot.

Rebecca had never been to Shooters, but it was easy to see that Shifters inhabited it. Harleys and old pickups filled the lot, and the men walking toward the rectangle of light that was the open door had the tall swagger of Shifter males. Mostly Lupines, Rebecca could tell from one sniff.

Walker dismounted the bike and made a show of helping her down, which was what a male groupie would do for his Shifter lady. Rebecca was dismayed by how much she liked his hands steadying her on her feet. This was getting dangerous fast.

Walker studied the other Shifters in the parking lot as he slid the fake ears onto his head. Then he drew a breath and settled into character. He took on the kind of slouch Rebecca had seen in the male groupies at Liam's bar, nonchalant and excited at the same time.

Weird to see Walker subsume his take-no-shit personality into that of a man who was smug he'd landed himself a Shifter woman. His stance both congratulated himself and dared anyone to try to take her away. That, and he was looking forward to her having her way with him later.

Wow. Rebecca cleared her throat, far more nervous than he was. "I guess we go inside," she said.

Walker didn't answer. He came to her, took her arm and draped it around his neck, hanging on to her hand. "*Now*, we go in," he said in a low voice. "Try to act like you're enjoying this."

She was, but not in the way he meant. "Right." Rebecca took a breath, as he had, and tried to behave as though she'd snared this hot guy and was going to put him through his paces all night.

The images that flashed through her head had her knees buckling. Walker steadied her, the strength in his grip astonishing. Then he marched her to the open door of the bar and inside to heat and noise.

CHAPTER TEN

Shooters was typical for a Shifter bar in South Texas. Rebecca had never been to this particular one—she never got out much beyond Austin and its environs—and so didn't worry too much about running into anyone she knew.

Though Shifters could legally move about the state, most of them stayed pretty close to home. Territory was a tricky thing. Humans had laid the boundaries of Shiftertowns, but Shifters knew where the true boundaries were.

Shiftertown leaders considered that the Shifters they'd been put in charge of were basically one extended pack, pride, or clan. Territories radiated out from each Shiftertown to where the leaders had agreed theirs ended and another leader's began. Humans might not be aware of these demarcations, but every Shifter knew them.

Shooters was outside the area that Liam and his father, Dylan, controlled. This bar would be under the purview of the Shiftertown on the western outskirts of Houston.

Rebecca had never met its leader, and she wasn't in a hurry to. She'd play it cool tonight. They'd listen, learn, and leave.

Walker's arm around her neck was solid and warm. The two were about the same height, his weight on her supporting rather than dragging. She slid her arm around his rock-hard waist under his coat, the intimacy of their half embrace making her breath come faster.

The entrance was lighted—Shifters liked to see who walked inside any building they were in—but beyond that, the bar proper was in near darkness.

Again, a territory thing. Newcomers would be disoriented for a few seconds from walking from bright to dark, while the Shifters inside could see clearly who'd entered. If the Shifters decided they were enemies, they'd be surrounded and thrown out.

Didn't matter that humans owned these bars. When Shifters decided they liked a place, they could have the humans doing what they wanted pretty quick. Those like Liam manipulated through charm and a lazy smile; others, like Dylan, did it by intimidation.

The Shifters here must not have worried about Rebecca and Walker, because no one charged them, no Collars sparked in the darkness. The two of them strolled, unhindered, into the wall of sound and darkness.

Rebecca's eyes adjusted quickly. Walker took a little more time, but he used their hold on each other to keep from tripping or running into anything without being obvious about it.

The music was a rapid staccato. In an area of country-western roadhouses, this bar was defiantly blasting rap.

Rebecca liked it, and started moving to the music before she realized it. She loved to dance.

She and Walker made for the bar, which was what people who came in here would do. Drinks first, then dancing.

The human bartender looked as though he could hold his own against Shifters. He had a craggy face, well-muscled tattooed arms, and hard eyes. Rebecca ordered beer for them both, Walker keeping very quiet as he looked around.

The bartender gave Walker a glance of disgust, clearly not liking groupies, especially not male ones. He slid both bottles toward Rebecca, took her cash, and gave her a grudging nod when she tipped him.

Walker lifted his bottle and turned his back to the bar. "Anyone here you know?" He stood very close so he only had to lean to her a little to speak into her ear.

"Not so far."

"Good. Let's make some new friends."

He waited for Rebecca to walk away first, like a good groupie would do. He was closely watching the few other male groupies in here, adjusting his gait to match theirs. He was good at subterfuge.

"Making new friends" apparently meant talking to other groupies, not Shifters. Reasonable—groupies would speak to those they wouldn't consider a threat. The young women eagerly eying the male Shifters were perfectly happy to move some of their attention to Walker. They recognized strength and a sexy man when they saw him.

At Walker's whispered suggestion, Rebecca left him to it and sauntered back to the bar, assessing the other Shifters along the way. She glanced at Walker from time to time, pretending to keep a jealous eye on him, which wasn't difficult to fake. The groupie girls were opening up to him, leaning in, touching his knee. If he wanted to take one of them home tonight, he'd only have to ask.

She noted that the Shifters here were relaxed, at ease, not too worried about anything. This was their go-to comfort place, like Liam's bar in Austin. If they ran a kidnapping ring, they weren't showing any sign of it.

The male Shifters had all focused on Rebecca as soon as she'd walked in the door, never mind she was with Walker. Shifter population was disproportionately male, and those males were always looking for mates. An unmated, unknown female, alone without her family, would be considered fair game.

The female Shifters in the bar regarded Rebecca without concern. Competition for mates was strongest among the males. Shifter females had their pick—not that they wouldn't fight to the death if two of them picked the same one.

The females were curious, though. Rebecca was out of her territory, she was a bear Shifter in a sea of Lupines and Felines, and they had to be wondering what she was doing.

"You are so out of place, girlfriend." A leggy Feline woman had left a laughing circle of friends to stroll to the bar and order another round. She could have remained seated and had one of the waitresses bring the drinks, but she'd come to scope out Rebecca.

Rebecca jerked her chin at Walker, deep in conversation with the eager young groupies. "He wanted to go somewhere new. Bored."

The Feline gave Walker an appreciative look, but shook her head. "Groupies. Why do you bother with them?"

Rebecca shrugged. "They don't go all alpha-male domination on me. That gets old."

The woman laughed. "Too right. I have three brothers."

"Yeah, well, you should try living with bears. I have to threaten to turn them into rugs to stop them being total shits."

The Feline woman laughed loudly. She was pretty, with a fine-boned face and blue eyes. Rebecca wondered what her wildcat was, but she wasn't good at judging Felines.

"Felines can be just as bad," the woman conceded. "Then there's Lupines. Eww." She wrinkled her nose, and Rebecca and she laughed and exchanged a high five. They could find common ground in cross-species rivalry.

"He's cute, though," the Feline said, looking at Walker as she lifted her beer bottle. "Tasty. I can see the attraction. If I were into groupies, I wouldn't mind one like that."

Rebecca gave her a nod. The Feline's deliberate use of the caveat signaled she'd back off Walker, not be a threat.

"There are a lot of groupies here," Rebecca said, glancing around the bar. They were mostly women, with a handful of men.

The Feline snorted. "That's because there are plenty of horny male Shifters to go around. The shitheads soak it up. Love the attention."

"Really?" The groupies seemed to be on one side of the room, Shifter men on the other. "I don't see much interaction."

"Oh, there will be later. Most of the time, though, the males simply eye them for hours, then cut one out of the herd and take her away."

"True love?" Rebecca asked, grinning. "Or true lust?"

"What do you think? Males go on and on about wanting to seek the mate bond and start having cubs, but as soon as a they see a woman with painted-on whiskers in a tight-ass skirt, they're on her like flies on sugar."

Rebecca laughed. "Yeah, same in my Shiftertown. They should have some shame. I might have a groupie in tow, but I don't go looking for a new one every night."

"Like I said, you have good taste, girlfriend." The Feline gave Walker another appreciative look. "He is *hot*."

Rebecca couldn't argue. Walker was in the center of an interested group of women, all smiles as he talked. She'd never seen the taciturn Walker open up so much. Watching him interacting so casually and easily burned a sharp pain in her chest.

The male Shifters were taking notice too. Belligerent stares raked over the tight circle of women and Walker, the groupies now paying no attention to the Shifters.

"Uh-oh," the Feline said. "You might just have to go rescue him."

"Damn it," Rebecca said in irritation. "Looks like." She thumped her bottle to the bar and began to move toward the clump of groupies Walker had enthralled.

Male Shifters had also started forward. Rebecca recognized their stride—arrogant alphas ready to throw out a trespasser, not gently.

Rebecca sped her steps, cutting across the paths of several Lupines whose eyes were beginning to glow white.

"Hey, sweetie," Rebecca said, making her voice sulky as she slid in front of Walker. Her position both blocked the advancing males and put herself between Walker and his new female friends. "What are you doing still sitting here? I came to dance."

"Oh, you don't have to worry about *him*," one of the groupies said, her smile wrinkling her painted-on cat's nose. "He's cool. He can't stop talking about you."

Walker sent Rebecca a smile that was both heart-melting and promised later sin. She knew he did it for show—what wouldn't she give for the promise to be real?

Walker rose to his feet with quick ease and put his hand on her elbow. "Sure, babe. Whatever you want."

"Bye, Walter!" one of the groupies said, and the others took up the cry. "Nice meeting you, Walter. Don't be a stranger."

"*Walter?*" Rebecca asked in his ear as he walked her away.

"Close enough that I'll naturally respond to the name, even if I forget I'm using it. Do you really want to dance?"

Rebecca loved to dance, but a few of the male Shifters had broken off from the main bunch and were following them.

"No, I think it's time to leave."

"Nope." Walker's hand on her elbow was firm. "I got some good intel. If we run away now, it will look like that's what we came for."

"If you hadn't noticed, three mean-looking Lupines are ready to teach you a lesson about poaching in their fishpond. If you fight them, you're blown. If *I* fight them, I'll kick their asses. Then they'll complain to their leader, Liam will have to talk to him, and—"

"Shut up, and come here."

Rebecca bit back her instinct to argue and let Walker

pull her into a hallway that led to a storage area and rear exit. Walker halted suddenly and slammed himself back against the wall. His grip on Rebecca pulled her hard against him, making it look as though she'd pinned *him*.

"Yell at me," he whispered.

"What? Oh . . ." Rebecca cleared her throat and spoke in a loud voice. "You came here with *me*, sweetie." She gave him a Kodiak bear snarl. "If you want a *Shifter*, you don't run after those pathetic excuses for women."

"Hey, baby, don't be mad." The catch in Walker's voice was just right. "You know I only want you."

Her heart squeezed again. Walker's eyes were half-closed, his baritone smooth and filled with the right amount of longing. *You know I only want you.*

No wonder those groupies had hung on his every word.

Growls filled the hall as one of the Lupines found them. He was alone—the others had likely turned back to secure their groupie of choice for the night.

The Lupine's Collar sparked. He was spoiling for a fight, never mind rules. Rebecca doubted anyone at this bar would call the cops on him—they were isolated here, and Shifters clearly had the upper hand.

Rebecca started to face the Lupine, to stare him down and figure out how to get out of this, but Walker jerked her back to him.

Her lips parted in surprise, then Walker's mouth landed against hers and locked into a hard kiss.

CHAPTER ELEVEN

The world stopped. Gone was the dingy smell of the back hall, the thumping noise from the bar, the gritty floor beneath Rebecca's feet.

She swore she was hanging in space, aware of nothing but the heat of Walker's body against hers, and his hands, and his mouth.

Walker's fingers curled on her jacket, keeping her close, but Rebecca wouldn't have been able to step away from him if she'd tried. He was her anchor, the only thing that prevented her floating away on a swirl of light and feeling.

She sank still more against him, caught and held by the hard strength of his body. His lips were smooth, his skilled mouth opening hers. She tasted beer, spice, a bite of heat.

Walker might have faked being a groupie, but he wasn't faking this kiss. He commanded with it, exploring and taking, but also giving. His lips moved, his mouth hot and strong. He was warmth; he was bone-melting desire.

Anything rigid inside Rebecca softened, until she was leaning hopelessly against him, body against body. Their clothes kept them apart, but the fabric couldn't shut out the vibrant need that thrummed from him to Rebecca and back again. Every desire she'd ever had for Walker poured forth, stealing her reason.

Her hands found his shoulders, hanging on, the muscle beneath his shirt living strength. Walker slid his grip from her jacket to her hips and pulled her closer with a fierce jerk.

She felt the hard ridge in his jeans, the betrayal that this embrace wasn't entirely for show. Walker wanted her without shame, his warmth wrapping her and willing her surrender.

"I should puke," someone snarled. A huge hand fell on Walker's shoulder, jerking him away from Rebecca.

Walker turned his face away so the Lupine wouldn't see the flash of fury in his eyes, but Rebecca caught it. She saw that Walker could kill the Lupine right now and stroll away without remorse.

Walker did nothing. He was a man who could control his rage, containing himself to do the job at hand.

Rebecca returned the Lupine's snarl with a growl of impatience. Walker had to act intimidated, but Rebecca couldn't afford to. "Go screw yourself. I'm busy."

The Lupine carefully didn't touch her, she noticed. He couldn't be sure she wouldn't turn bear and smack him down, or that the rest of her clan wouldn't come down on his ass for doing something stupid. Clans were very protective.

Humans on the other hand, he obviously had no use for. The Lupine's grip tightened on Walker's shoulder, though Walker still carefully didn't look at him.

"You're fair game," the Lupine said to Rebecca. "A female in your fertile years, blasting mating frenzy everywhere. So why are you here with this dickhead?" He gave Walker a shake.

Walker had so much cold anger in his eyes that Rebecca was surprised the pipes next to him didn't freeze. He remained stolid, pretending to be too afraid to fight back, but if the Lupine had seen his expression, it would have scared him shitless.

"I didn't notice anything else I wanted in this bar," Rebecca said. She'd sized up the Lupine—he was fairly dominant, but not top of his pack. Maybe second or third. Arrogant enough to think he could get away with whatever he felt like.

Rebecca, on the other hand, was alpha female in her clan—not that there were any other adult female bears in her clan at the Austin Shiftertown. She refused to show any kind of submission to an effing Lupine, no matter how special he thought he was.

The Lupine must have realized this, so he turned his hostility on Walker. "You like subbing to Shifters, groupie? How about you spend the rest of this conversation on your knees?"

The look on Walker's face changed from suppressed anger to determination. He'd reached the end of his rope. Rebecca took a few discreet steps back, giving him room for whatever he planned to do.

Walker bowed his head and dropped to the floor, the little *thump* of his knees meeting concrete audible over the music behind them. He threw off the Lupine's hand at the same time, as though indicating he was happy to bow to Rebecca, but not to another Shifter.

The Lupine snarled at him and drew back his fist to punch Walker in the face. Rebecca reached to catch the Lupine's arm, but Walker yelled at her, "Don't touch him!"

At the same time, she heard a swift buzz of electricity. Rebecca jumped back as Walker's Taser fired into the Lupine's chest. The Lupine's body vibrated with the sudden shock, his wolf eyes widening. His Collar sparked, white lights in the darkness, and then the Lupine crashed to the floor, dragging a crate of empty bottles with him.

Walker clamped his hand around Rebecca's and pulled her out the back door, tucking his Taser into his jacket as he ran.

Rebecca sprinted with him toward her motorcycle, expecting any minute for Shifters to pour out of the bar, ready to teach the outsiders a lesson. But the door that had swung shut behind them remained that way. Maybe the noise had drowned out the altercation, or maybe the Lupine's friends didn't give a rat's ass if he got trounced.

Rebecca didn't linger and find out. She was on her bike, Walker swinging on behind, and she started up and peeled out.

A few miles down the highway, Walker tapped her arm and pointed to a gas station coming up on the side of the road. Rebecca pulled in and around the building, halting in the quiet back lot. She killed the engine and hopped off after he did.

She pulled her helmet from her head and dragged in a breath of chilly night air tainted with gasoline fumes. "Shit, Walker. You took a Taser into a Shifter bar?"

Walker shrugged, scrubbing his hand through his short hair. "Never know when I'm going to need it. Security in that place isn't exactly tight."

"No." Rebecca dragged in another breath, then she laughed. "Wonder if he'll remember what happened when he wakes up?"

"Probably. And he might come looking for us, so we shouldn't linger in the neighborhood. One of the groupies told me about another place that's worth checking out."

He started to put on his helmet, but Rebecca stilled his hand. She brought out a couple of tissues from her pocket. "You're smeared."

She dabbed where their kiss had sent the paint Mabel had so carefully applied into the creases around his mouth.

Walker's light blue eyes softened like mist in moonlight. "Becks," he said.

"Yeah?" She kept dabbing.

"Don't . . ." He tried to turn his face away, and she stood still, her heart beating swiftly, hurting. Walker looked back into her eyes, his chest lifting with a sharp breath. "Damn it," he whispered.

He laced his fingers behind her neck and dragged her against him, the helmet in his hand pressing hard into her back.

This kiss was as fierce, as earthshattering as the last. Walker's hand on the back of her neck was firm, nothing submissive about it. He'd finished with playacting.

His mouth opened hers, and Rebecca responded with need. Hunger.

As before, the world swirled away, leaving nothing but him and her, the warmth of his skin, damp with sweat, the scent of the night on him. She had no awareness of breathing or standing, only being held by this beautiful man, his mouth working on hers.

His hair was prickly under her fingers, the short buzz tickling. He knew how to kiss—tasting every corner of her mouth, fingers practiced at holding her in place. He'd been closer to her in the hallway, but the line of his thighs against hers, the press of the helmet locking her to him, made her shake.

Walker eased back from the searing kiss, his breath coming fast. Rebecca opened her eyes to find his crystal blue ones staring into hers.

His voice was a rumble in the night. "I've wanted to do that for so long."

Rebecca should return with a quip, or ask, *Then why haven't you?* But her tongue was heavy in her mouth, and words wouldn't form. She couldn't even answer what she truly thought, *So have I.*

Walker only looked at her, his granite-hard face softened by shadows. "I want to make love to you."

Her brain's response was, *Oh, goody!* What came out of her mouth was, "Gunh?"

One corner of his mouth twitched. "Was that a yes?"

"I . . . We . . . Um . . ."

Great. Rebecca who could make any Shifter nervous by walking by him, who could defeat hulking alpha males with her sly suggestiveness, was tongue-tied by the man she'd give anything to be with.

She cleared her throat. "It's a little greasy here."

Walker's laugh was warm and velvet, like the darkness

around them. "I didn't mean right now. Later. In a bed. A big one with lots of room. Pillows. Champagne—no wait, I'd rather have beer."

"Me too."

"It's a date, then. We get done with this, we find a mattress and a lot of privacy."

"Okay." Rebecca's knees were trembling so much she was amazed she could stand.

Walker's gaze was on hers again, his smile fading, a frown pulling his brows together. The paint had smeared on his nose, whiskers blurred from their kisses. The lines around his eyes were still solid, but a few trickles of black made tears among the white foundation.

He should look ridiculous, but he didn't at all as he cupped Rebecca's face, thumb tracing her cheek.

Without speaking, Walker leaned to her again, his lips warm in the chill. Rebecca latched her fingers around the lapels of his leather coat, the only thing keeping her upright as her mouth sought his.

Nothing mattered for that glittering moment, only Walker kissing her in the darkness, his body hard against hers.

I want to make love to you. How did he know that the blatant statement was the way to seduce her—no teasing, no hints, no waiting for her to understand?

No, he was exactly what she needed. A man who knew what he wanted and wasn't afraid to say so.

Her heart bumped and raced as she pulled him closer. His mouth was a point of heat, and Rebecca clung to him, the only thing solid in her dissolving world . . .

A growl sounded in the darkness. "Goddess and God, get a room."

The voice that boomed at them was Lupine, but she recognized it. Broderick.

He strode toward them from around the corner of the station, his usual scowl in place. Walker raised his head but didn't take his arms from around Rebecca. No embarrassment. He simply watched Broderick approach, while Rebecca's heart pounded, and she resisted the urge to wipe her wet mouth.

A young woman with short, dark hair walked at Broderick's side. Joanne. He'd been protective of her since she'd come to Shiftertown searching for her sister. They weren't having sex—Shifters would have scented it if so, and spread that gossip—but Joanne had become friends with him, if Broderick could have anything as civilized as friends.

Broderick folded his arms, his hooded sweat jacket stretching over his wide shoulders. "Seriously, Becks? With someone from Shifter Bureau? That's just wrong."

"Not your business, Broderick," Rebecca said with a warning growl.

Walker completely ignored Broderick. "Joanne," he said, easing away from Rebecca. "Good, I'm glad you came. You need to hear this too."

The man cared less that an angry, dominant Lupine Shifter stood two feet away from him. His words and stance broadcast that, to him, the most important person in this conversation was Joanne. Joanne responded to him, ignoring the warning glares Rebecca and Broderick were giving each other.

"You found something out about Nancy?" Joanne had a

cute, almost triangular face and large brown eyes, which were now filled with hope.

"Not exactly," Walker said. "But I learned a couple things that might point in the right direction. The women I talked to mentioned a place they said was 'way cooler' than Shooters, in their words. A place with more exciting Shifter action. Not all of them were comfortable talking about it, and some outright said they were afraid to go. The Shifters in wherever they meant, I deduced from their hints, are wilder and more, as they said, 'interesting.'"

Rebecca gave a short laugh. "I bet the a-hole you tased would be seriously unhappy if he knew the groupies found other Shifters more interesting."

"Same thing ran through my mind." Walker shoved his hands into his pockets. "The Shifters we just left were off the leash, so to speak. Their leader hasn't pounded into them that they shouldn't stir up trouble with humans, even groupies. But a few of those women found *them* too tame."

"Wait," Broderick broke in. "You tased a Shifter? Who the hell do you . . ." He trailed off and looked thoughtful. "No, wait. I wish I could have seen that. I swear, only dick-brains go to Shooters."

"So I might have been right after all," Joanne said, ignoring Broderick. "Shifters really could have kidnapped Nancy. I was just scoping out the wrong Shifters."

"We don't know that yet," Walker said. "We need to be cautious about this. They can't see us coming—abductors spook easily if they think someone is closing in on them." He left hanging what happened to the abductee in that case, but they all could guess. "And these Shifters might not know anything about it."

"I say we find this place and kick ass until we do know," Broderick said. "They won't suspect anything if I go in. They'll just think I'm restless and want a fight. Which, you know, isn't wrong."

Rebecca shook her head. "We can't turn a Shifter bar into a fight club. Liam would be all over you for that, and so would whatever Shiftertown leader whose territory we'll be in."

Broderick started to argue, fists balled, but Joanne stepped in front of him and faced Walker. "Can we at least go check it out?"

"I plan to," Walker said. "We're not going all the way back to Austin yet."

Joanne let out her breath and gave him a smile. "Thanks," she said.

Two conversations were happening here, Rebecca realized. The two humans were communicating about what was more important to them than anything else, including personal safety—finding Nancy. Broderick and Rebecca were on a different plane—weighing how to deal with Shifters who might be less inhibited, and how to protect Walker and Joanne from them.

Who was right at this moment—the humans or the Shifters?

"Did they give you directions?" Rebecca asked.

"They did." Walker's gaze met hers, his eyes holding both anticipation and remembered warmth of their kiss.

Broderick made an impatient noise. "Then what are we waiting for?" He grabbed Joanne's hand and strode away with her, back to the gleam of his motorcycle at the edge of the lot.

"Want me to drive?" Walker asked Rebecca.

Rebecca stepped close to him, put her hand on his chest, and daringly gave him a kiss on the lips. Then she turned away and tossed him her keys as she headed for the bike. "Be my guest."

CHAPTER TWELVE

————

The Shifter bar the groupies had directed Walker to lay almost straight south of San Antonio. Towns thinned out once they left the I-10 between San Antonio and Houston, growing sparser as Walker steered Rebecca's motorcycle down a two-lane highway that stretched into darkness.

Rebecca's strong arms wrapped him from behind, her body soft against him as they balanced together. He already loved riding with her, never wanted to stop.

Walker was breaking his own rules right and left, especially the one about mixing sexual pleasure with an op. He completed the mission first—*then* he could go out and celebrate with a beautiful woman.

He'd done covert missions with women before, including one in which he pretended to be the husband of a female operative, but they'd been totally professional. The woman had been married to another guy anyway. After the mission, her husband had joined them for after-mission revelry at a bar. The woman had walked away arm-in-arm with her husband, and Walker had gone home alone.

Easier to feel nothing in a job like his. He'd seen too much death, too much cruelty for the sake of it. Better to live in a black-and-white world—do the job, celebrate a victory or survive a defeat, go home and sleep.

What had begun as a way to keep himself sane had grown into habit, and now he didn't know any other way.

Kissing Rebecca in the hall to keep the Shifters from catching on to what they were doing had broken open something inside him. He fought like hell to contain it, but it was too late.

The moment he'd wrapped his arms around her and dragged her against him, Walker had known he'd screwed up. He hadn't wanted to let go. One taste of her, and he was doomed—he'd always known he would be. She wound him up like no other woman had, and not just because she was Shifter. She was *Rebecca*.

After this—after this . . . Hell, if there was an after this, he'd take her to bed, as he'd told her. Once, at the very least. They knew each other now, they could toast their success with drinks and a night of intense pleasure.

Walker knew, though, as Rebecca adjusted her hold, her hands warm in the darkness, that once with her would never be enough.

Walker leaned into a turn that took them to an even smaller road leading out into emptiness. Broderick's head-lamp behind him cut into the night as Broderick followed with Joanne perched behind him.

The bar Walker sought lay four more miles down this highway, outside a town that was all but dried up. The town's main crossroads didn't even have a stoplight, its main intersection marked with a faded stop sign shot through with bullet holes. Walker and Broderick rode past the few houses, most of them boarded up, and out the other side of the town. The roadhouse was a mile and a half from there.

Not as many vehicles filled this lot, but that didn't mean the place was empty. Most were pickups, and a group could have piled into each.

Walker parked in darkness out of sight from the front door—this one closed—and turned off the engine. Broderick pulled up behind him, his engine throbbing louder than any needed to, even a Harley's. But that was Broderick.

Joanne pulled off her helmet as Broderick shut down his bike. This parking lot had no lights—the only illumination came from the floodlight over the front door. Joanne looked scared; Rebecca, impatient and edgy.

Broderick started to stride to the door, but Walker reached out and pulled him back.

Broderick instantly swung around, Collar sparking, fist coming at him. Walker grabbed the fist in a competent hand and twisted Broderick's arm around in a move that could break a human bone. Broderick jerked away, more angry than hurt.

"Stop it," Rebecca said before Broderick could try again. "Walker's right. We don't rush in. We check it out. Stay in character."

"They're *Shifters*," Broderick growled. "They don't get *character*. They understand *fight or fuck off*."

"Please." Joanne touched Broderick's wrist. "If they know where my sister is—if my sister is anywhere near here —I want to find out without tipping them off."

The change in Broderick was amazing. When Walker had grasped Broderick's arm, he'd turned into a crazed, fighting beast. When Joanne did, all the belligerence left his eyes, and he gave her a look that was almost tender.

"I know you're scared for her, sweetie," Broderick said, caressing her hand. "Don't worry. We'll find her." Oblivious to the interested glances Walker and Rebecca exchanged, Broderick let out a breath. "All right, we'll try the *covert* way for now. But if that doesn't work, I'm charging in there."

"If I need you, I'll yell," Walker said, less than patient. "Ready, Becks?"

Broderick snorted. "Goddess, she lets you call her Becks . . ."

Walker had already gripped Rebecca's upper arm and was guiding her toward the building. He heard Broderick's guffaw in the background, and Joanne's soft, *"Broderick."*

The door to this roadhouse was less welcoming than the last. The one at Shooters had at least been open. A spotlight threw a hard circle of yellow light around the doorstep and a few feet beyond, so that any Shifter looking out could see who stood there. The door itself was a slab of metal, gray, dinged with bullet holes, and rusted.

Walker hadn't been told about a secret knock or any such thing, but it didn't matter. As soon as Rebecca stepped into the light and reached for the door, it was pulled open.

Doors of drinking establishments were supposed to open outward—in case of fire, people could get out without the crowd crushing the doors shut. This one had been rehinged to open inward, so that the bouncer who answered it could use it to shove unwanted patrons out.

This particular bouncer was big, almost bear-sized, but

he wasn't a bear Shifter. Feline, Walker was certain. The man's light green eyes had the piercing stare of a cat, and his stance was edgy. Under the light, his round pupils flicked to feline-like slits and back again.

"No," the Feline said abruptly.

Walker stood a yard or so behind Rebecca, not only to pretend he was her groupie in tow, but to keep his face averted and in shadow. There was something wrong here, and his instinct was to hide any features this guy might recognize later.

Rebecca stared into the Feline's eyes without fear. "*No?* What does that mean? I heard this place was hot." She tried to look past the bouncer into the bar, but he'd positioned himself squarely in the door's opening.

"Bear," the Feline said.

"No shit," Rebecca returned. "You're a wildcat. We can recognize each other, so what? I just want a drink. Maybe some dancing."

The man's gaze moved to Rebecca's Collar and rested there. "What Shiftertown you from?"

He had a Texas drawl. Few Shifters had originated in the United States, except some of the Lupine clans—most bears came from Canada or, like Rebecca and Ronan, from Alaska. Felines, on the other hand, descended from clans in Europe, Ireland, and Scotland, with some, like Spike, from Mexico and on into South America. This meant that the Feline's South Texas accent had been acquired; probably he used it to obscure his origins for whatever reason.

"Does it matter?" Rebecca snapped in answer to his question.

"Not a lot of bears down here," the bouncer said. "You from Austin?"

If she lied, he'd scent it. If she chose not to answer, he might slam the door. Rebecca decided to go with the truth. "Yes. I felt like—"

"Dylan's Shiftertown." The Feline spat on the doorstep. Rebecca held her ground, but her back stiffened.

"Liam's now. Dylan retir—"

The Feline cut her off by taking a step back and slamming the door. Rebecca stared at the slab of metal before she growled, "Asshole."

Walker knew there was no way to get that door open again without a battering ram or explosives. No light shone through the bullet holes, which meant pistols and shotguns hadn't been able to penetrate it.

Rebecca was quivering with rage, but Walker touched her shoulder, signaling her to follow him away.

"Guess that didn't work," Broderick said as they reconvened in the darkness by the bikes. "Kicking ass is better."

"Shut up, Broderick," Rebecca growled, then she stopped, her gaze focusing on nothing as she thought. "Wait a sec. I was trying so hard to see around the guy, I didn't pay attention, but . . . Oh, wow." She snapped her head around to look at Walker, her brown eyes almost glowing in the darkness. "That's not right."

"What?" Broderick demanded, but Walker realized at the same moment what Rebecca meant.

Walker had noted every single thing about the bouncer, as the Feline and Rebecca had sized each other up, his subconscious tucking away the information until needed.

Now one glaring fact surfaced, dancing to the front of Walker's brain.

"He wasn't wearing a Collar," Rebecca said. "Not a real one, anyway."

That took a few heartbeats to sink in.

"Maybe he had it removed," Joanne said. "Broderick told me some Shifters are able to do that now."

Rebecca's fists clenched. "He *told* you? Goddess, Broderick. What does the phrase *Shifter secrets* mean to you?"

Broderick scowled back. "She's safe. She won't run out and blab it."

Joanne stood her ground under Rebecca's glare. "He's right, I won't," she said. "Broderick and his family have done a lot for me—do you think I'd do anything to hurt them?"

Rebecca threw up her hands and shook her head, but Walker interrupted. "It's a good guess, Joanne, but I don't think so. Only a few Shifters have had it done so far. The Collar moved on his neck and I didn't see a line underneath—when the Collar comes out of the skin, it leaves a red scar, and we don't know yet how long that takes to heal." He went silent a moment before he finished, "Which might mean that Shifter has never had a Collar on him."

They all went deadly silent, thinking it through.

"How can he not have a Collar?" Rebecca asked quietly.

Walker shrugged. "Not every Shifter got rounded up twenty years ago. According to Shifter Bureau records, some eluded capture. Hunters killed a lot of those, but there were Shifters who managed to escape. Like that guy who moved to Mexico and called himself Miguel. He set up a mock Shiftertown for un-Collared Shifters," he added for Joanne's benefit, in case she hadn't heard the story.

"Yeah, and they all went feral," Rebecca said. "They captured females, both Shifter and human—and had a good old time until their building got blown up."

Broderick chuckled. "I wish I could have seen that."

"This Feline wasn't feral," Rebecca pointed out. "Ferals stink. They don't like to wear clothes, and they don't have jobs. This guy obviously bathes and goes to work every night—a human has to own the bar and must have hired him, so there has to be some kind of record on him."

"Plus, he sounds like he knows who lives in what Shifter-town," Walker said. "Something a feral wouldn't care about. Are all the Shifters in there like him? Or is he an aberration?"

"Arrest him," Broderick said. "You're Shifter Bureau. It's your job to look for rogue Shifters and cage them. Go on. Tase him. Call in the choppers. Drag him off. "

"We aren't here about him," Rebecca said. "We're here to find Joanne's sister."

Broderick's growl rumbled in his throat. "Maybe it's all connected. Did you think of that?"

"It's connected," Walker broke in. "Somehow. We just have to find out how. Broderick, let me borrow your hoodie."

Broderick started. "What for? I don't want my clothes stinking of human. Not *male* human anyway." He added with a glance at Joanne.

Walker tugged tissues out of his pocket and started wiping the corners of his eyes. "He didn't get a good look at me. He was much more worried about Rebecca and who she was. In the hoodie, with my makeup changed, he might not realize I'm the same guy. Your scent will disguise mine, as well, in case he got a whiff of me. He'll think I'm a Lupine lover."

Rebecca swung to him. "'Scuse me . . . you're thinking of going in there alone?"

"Not alone. With Joanne. I'll bet they don't let in Shifters who aren't vetted, but I'm willing to risk they'll let in humans, especially groupies."

"No!" Broderick said, at the same time Rebecca growled, "Bad idea."

"No, it's a good idea," Joanne interrupted. "Let him have the jacket, Broderick. Walker can keep me safe. I am *not* leaving without more information about my sister."

The determination in her voice, and the hint of tears behind that, won the argument. Broderick, grumbling, stripped off his jacket.

Rebecca still didn't like it, Walker could see, but she helped him. With the aid of a flashlight and one of her bike's mirrors, they wiped off the Egyptian-like eye makeup and redrew his whiskers, attempting to make him look more Lupine-oriented than Feline.

Joanne had brought cat's ears for herself in case she had to go into one of the clubs, and she borrowed the eyeliner pencil to do a quick job on her own face.

When they were done, Walker encased himself in Broderick's hoodie, using it to hide his hair and put his face in shadow. He squeezed Rebecca's hand, and told her what he wanted her to do. She did not look happy, but she nodded, giving his hand a warm squeeze in return.

Then Walker released Rebecca, put his arm around Joanne's shoulders, and for the second time that night, approached the shot-up door of the roadhouse.

CHAPTER THIRTEEN

W alker had learned a long time ago that a person could make him- or herself look very different, especially in bad lighting, by changing posture, attitude, and one or two pieces of clothing. Extras in movies could play many parts by avoiding being seen too clearly by the cameras.

Walker slouched beside Joanne, making himself look lanky and loose and a little shorter than he truly was. He kept his eyes averted when the bouncer opened the door, so the man couldn't get a good look at them.

It also helped that he was a different bouncer, a Lupine this time. He had wiry black hair, tatts all over his arms, and light gray eyes. He, like the Feline, wore a fake Collar, with no evidence he'd ever had a real one.

The Lupine looked Joanne over, taking in her cat's ears and makeup but also her tight shirt and leather pants. "Hey, sweetie," he said to her. "You're cute, but I can't let you in until I know how you heard about this place."

Walker answered for her. Shifters could smell a lie, so Walker gave him the truth. "In a bar called Shooters." He made his voice thin and higher-pitched than his normal one. "They said it was wilder here."

The Lupine showed his teeth in a smile. "Yeah, we're wilder, definitely. Newbies stick to the left side of the bar. Got it? And you need this." He reached for Joanne's hand and rubbed the back of his thumb hard over it.

Walker repressed his instinct to spring to her aid, realizing that the Lupine was spreading his scent on Joanne's skin. Better than an ink stamp.

Walker let the Lupine rub his hand as well, then the bouncer stood back and let them in.

This roadhouse was darker than the other, with only a few lights over the bar and on signs pointing out emergency exits. Shifters could see pretty well in the dark and didn't need too much light. Humans here would have to live with it, but Walker had a feeling they didn't mind.

The left side of the bar had mostly empty tables, with humans in groupie makeup clumped together. Must be the newbies. The rest of the bar was full of women and men in full groupie mode, surrounded by plenty of Shifters.

The Shifters were Felines and Lupines. Walker had spent enough time with Ronan and family to recognize bears, and none of these were. Some were in animal form—a few leopards wandered around, along with a big, shaggy wolf. One wildcat lay with his feet in a groupie's lap, and she was stroking his head. If the music hadn't been so loud, Walker would bet he'd hear the wildcat purring.

Walker led Joanne to the tables with the newbies. Better to follow the rules for now.

The young women here were a little more reticent, but they opened up a little when Walker said hello in a friendly way, and Joanne did her best to look cute and harmless. Walker noticed more male groupies here than the other place, though there weren't that many female Shifters.

"Our first time too," one of the girls said. "I'm loving it." She looked more terrified than excited, in Walker's opinion. She leaned forward and whispered, as though keeping her words away from Shifter hearing. "The Shifters don't wear real Collars."

"That's what makes it fun," a second young woman said. "They're not controlled by anyone. They're truly wild. They could do *anything*."

As with her friend, what was in her eyes said different things from her words. Walker guessed that hearing about Shifters who could do anything was exciting in theory, but now that the women were here, watching the dangerous Shifters walk around, it was scary as hell.

"How do they not get caught?" Walker asked, also in a whisper.

"No one tells," one of the young men said. He had his face painted similar to the way Walker had worn his originally tonight. "They mark us with their scent, and they can find us if they think we'll betray them. But anyway, why would we? We love Shifters. Shifters should be free."

Walker agreed with him on the last part but, he hoped, without the fanatic light in the young man's eyes.

These Shifters, however, weren't doing anything Walker hadn't seen Shifters *with* Collars do. They drank beer, shouted to one another, were arrogant shits. Some had arms draped around groupies' shoulders, the few female Shifters had males hovering protectively near them.

The difference showed itself when two Lupines got into a fight. The bone of contention, a groupie woman in a wisp of a dress that fastened at one shoulder, screamed and scrambled out of the way as the Lupines attacked each other full force.

Both Shifters and groupies boiled away from the two Lupines as they tumbled over tables, shifting as they went. It was like being at the fight club, except with no boundary ring, no rules, no referees. Shifters stood back and watched, not attempting to help or break it up.

Fur flew and soon enough, so did blood. No one stopped them. Walker rose to watch, as the other groupies did, and he stood tensely. Part of his job was to contain something like this, to keep Shifters in line. That's why he carried a Taser in his pocket and a tranq gun in his truck.

He knew, though, that if he marched over and tased the two combatants, he wouldn't make it out alive. Joanne might not either.

The Lupines in wolf form rolled to the middle of the floor, biting, writhing, clawing. They moved so fast they were one ball of fur, doing their best to rip each other open.

This would be a fight to the death—Walker saw that. His heart pumped furiously, but at the same time, his training took over, turning his fight-or-flight adrenaline into cold strength.

He took in the building and the exits. If he could get the two outside, he could bring them both down with the Taser before anyone was the wiser. He might be able to turn the situation into an opportunity for getting answers as well.

As Walker planned his strategy for driving them toward the nearest emergency exit, one of the fighting Lupines yelped and went limp.

Now other Shifters moved, five of them, including the two bouncers, lifting the victor off the loser before he could rip out the loser's throat.

The winner lifted his head and howled. He shifted, becoming a blood-coated, naked human, tight body covered with tatts. He spit on the wolf who lay motionlessly on the floor, called him a filthy name, and sauntered over to the young woman they'd fought over. He grabbed her by the dress and dragged her up his bloody body for a kiss.

Walker had his hand inside his jacket, around the Taser, but the woman came out of the kiss all smiles. She stroked his arm.

The winner, still naked, had obviously grown excited by the fight. He wrapped his arm around the woman and pulled her through a dark door that was not an exit.

The wolf who'd lost lay in a pool of blood. He wasn't dead, because when the Lupine bouncer tried to move him, he groaned. The Lupine looked over to the groupies near Walker, pointed to one of the young women Walker had been talking to, and beckoned her over.

The woman looked terrified. Walker rose with her, made a motion for Joanne to stay put, and escorted the young woman to the middle of the room.

The Lupine snarled at Walker. "I didn't ask for you. He needs the touch of a woman."

"I'm a medic," Walker said. "In real life."

The Lupine sniffed in his direction, decided Walker was telling the truth, and gave him a brief nod. Walker helped the Lupine lift the wolf, who snarled softly, and carry him to a deserted corner. The groupie woman followed, uncertain.

The Lupine shook the other wolf when they laid him on the floor. "Can you hear me, Tev? Shift back."

The wolf groaned again, the groan ending in a whimper. Slowly the wolf morphed back to human—agonizingly slowly. Walker heard his bones and cartilage crackling as he changed shape.

A few minutes later, Walker looked at a young man who couldn't be more than Scott's age, say late twenties, still very young for a Shifter. Walker guessed the Shifter was just past his Transition. So what was he doing picking fights with older Shifters in a bar in the middle of nowhere?

Whatever the reason, the kid was in bad shape. "I'll need water, clean cloths, and whatever kind of first-aid kit you have. Gauze would be good, and needle and thread." Walker gently touched the young man's shin. "And a splint."

"Shifters heal fast," the Lupine growled.

"Not that fast. And they need to heal correctly. Do you have the stuff?"

The note in Walker's voice made the Lupine shoot him a sharp look. Groupies didn't give orders, and Walker had done it automatically, in a tone that said he expected to be obeyed. Now to see if the Lupine would kill him with one blow, or go get the first-aid kit.

The Lupine huffed a breath, gripped the female groupie's shoulder, and said, "You, come and help me."

Walker was left alone with the young Shifter. "What's your name?" he asked.

"Tevis," the Lupine answered, his voice a whisper.

"I'm Walter," Walker said, deciding to continue with the

name. "What the hell are you doing here, challenging a Shifter twice your age and experience?"

Tevis managed a little smile. "Wanted . . . mate."

Walker thought about the young woman in the dress that could dissolve in a high wind, her smile at the winning Shifter, and her blatant unconcern for the loser. "Don't worry about her. You can do better."

"Pretty," Tevis said, sounding wistful.

"Looks aren't everything." Not that Walker could cease thinking about Rebecca's brown eyes, the delicious curve of her body, her beautiful face.

"I'm going to touch you," Walker said. "I'm checking for breaks and to see how bad you are. All right?"

"I'm fine," Tevis snapped, but so weakly the words barely sounded over the noise of the bar.

"No, you're not." Walker put careful but competent hands on the Shifter's bare legs. The right shin was definitely broken. "Let me tell you about women, big guy," he said as he went on with the examination. "You want one with a good heart. Looks don't last. A good heart is forever."

He should talk. He'd taken one look at the gorgeous package of Rebecca, and his world had changed.

"Not a lot of choice," Tevis said.

"Is that what all the Shifters in this bar are doing? Looking for mates?"

Tevis shrugged. "Good a place as any."

The young Lupine wore a fake Collar. As Walker ran his fingers around Tevis's neck, he found bite wounds from the fight, but no crease or scars that a real Collar would have left when removed.

"How did you not get rounded up?" Walker asked him

quietly. He rubbed the kid's neck. "You're not like other Shifters."

"Mother hid me," Tevis said. "They took her. Never found me. I was just a cub. Almost went feral. I finally came across others like me."

"In South Texas?" Walker asked. Didn't sound too likely.

"Minnesota, by the Canadian border. We came down here a couple years ago." Tevis smiled. "For the weather."

"How did you all find each other? Do you have a leader?"

"No. Word gets around."

No leader sounded even more unlikely. Shifters always had an alpha in charge, even if it was just one person heading a small family. The idea that a group of Shifters could come together without someone in charge was odd—and for Shifters, dangerous. Or maybe Walker wasn't asking the right questions.

He couldn't ask more, though, because the bouncer and groupie returned a moment later.

The bouncer shoved the young woman down beside Tevis and dropped a first-aid kit and some Ace bandages next to Walker. "Fix him. If you can't, tell me."

Fear flickered in Tevis's eyes. Walker wondered what would happen to Tevis if he couldn't be helped. Would they put him down like a hurt dog? With a drug? Or a bullet?

"I'll fix him," Walker said, giving Tevis a reassuring look. "I'm good at it."

The bouncer turned away but didn't go far. He stood with his back to them, watching the rest of the bar, but was close enough that he'd be able to hear conversation and be back to them in two steps.

The groupie woman started to cry. "I can't do this. I can't."

No, she couldn't, Walker realized. She'd come here to party and hook up with a Shifter, not be a makeshift nurse to a Shifter who might not survive.

He called to the bouncer. "Let her go. My friend can help me."

The bouncer did not look happy, but he saw that the crying girl was going to be useless. He lifted her to her feet, pushed her back toward the tables, and gestured for Joanne to come.

Joanne scuttled over, afraid but determined. Walker silenced her with a look and continued to minister to Tevis. The bouncer watched them for a time then moved off to keep an eye on the bar again.

Walker wished he had a splint, but he had to make do with the thick Ace bandage and a long piece of hard plastic that had once been the lid to something.

"This is going to hurt," Walker said to Tevis. "There aren't any painkillers. You really should be at a hospital."

"Can't," Tevis said, grinning weakly. "Bad idea."

If hospital staff realized that Tevis was a Shifter with a fake Collar, they'd report him in a heartbeat.

"I understand." Walker straightened the bad leg and told Joanne to be ready. "What happens when one of you is seriously hurt? Do you have a healer?"

Tevis shook his head. "If it's that bad, the Shifter dies. Gets turned to dust."

"You have a Guardian?" Walker asked in surprise. The Guardian of a Shifter's pack or clan had a Fae-made sword that would render a dead Shifter dust when the blade was thrust through his heart. Shifters believed this was the only route to the Summerland, the afterlife.

Tevis looked suddenly worried, as though he'd said too much. Groupies would know about Guardians, because they knew everything about Shifters. But an un-Collared Guardian still living wild? Walker wasn't sure how that could happen, how one could remain undetected.

Guardians had a computer database they called the Guardian Network, through which they both stored facts about all Shifters and communicated with one another. The language used to code it was ancient Fae, and no one but Guardians fully comprehended it. Most of them were accomplished hackers, or soon became such.

The Guardians were the keepers of knowledge—it would be highly unusual for a Guardian to be off that grid, and for the others to not know about him. Yet the few Guardians Walker had met had never mentioned an un-Collared Guardian running around in the world.

Walker tucked the fact away and got down to the business of getting Tevis's leg into the makeshift splint. He had Joanne hold everything steady while he took hold of Tevis's ankle, and in one hard jerk, aligned the bone.

Tevis yelled, and his wolf started to come. The bouncer swung back, concern and anger in his eyes.

Joanne quickly put her arm around Tevis. "It's all right. It's all right." She rubbed his chest. "He's fixing you."

She'd learned, it seemed, that touch helped Shifters deal with pain and heal. Just as Rebecca had held and calmed Scott last night at the arena, Joanne soothed Tevis back from the shift. Tevis sank against her, his head on her shoulder.

The leg was straight now. Walker wrapped it quickly

and competently, hoping that the swift-healing Shifter metabolism would kick in and fuse the bones by tomorrow.

Tevis leaned against Joanne as she put both arms around him. "Thanks," he said breathlessly. He sounded embarrassed.

Walker finished up, cleaning Tevis's bite wounds and applying gauze. The bouncer was watching them closely again.

"He should go home," Walker said, wadding up the cloths he'd used and unfolding to his feet. "Does he have family? Or friends who can help him?"

The bouncer started to answer, then scowled, as though realizing he'd been about to give away too much. "We'll take care of him. You two are done. Out."

Walker slid back into his groupie persona. "What? Why? We just got here."

"Another night." The bouncer clamped his hand on Walker's shoulder. "You say a word about what you've seen here, and you're dead meat. Understand? We'll know."

"I won't," Walker said quickly. "We get it. We want you to be free."

The bouncer gave him a little shake. "Good."

Joanne started to rise, but Tevis grabbed her hand. "Don't go. Let her stay." He turned wide, scared eyes to the bouncer. *"Please."*

The bouncer looked as though he didn't like making these kinds of decisions, but he sighed and gave Tevis a nod. "All right. She stays with him." He pointed at Walker. "You. Go."

Not good. Walker couldn't leave Joanne in here with these Shifters. Way too dangerous.

The bouncer saw Walker's indecision, and his voice hardened. "She *stays*. The cub needs her. She leaves when he's better."

"I'm *not* a cub," Tevis growled in protest. "I'm past my Transition."

The bouncer ignored him. "Don't worry about the girl," he said to Walker. "I'll watch out for her."

"It's all right," Joanne said. She sank back down to Tevis. "I don't mind. If I can help him, I want to stay."

She meant she wanted to find out if these Shifters knew anything about her sister. Walker understood that, but at the same time, leaving a civilian behind enemy lines was not what he did.

But, this wasn't a military campaign. This was a retrieval, though they had to find the target to retrieve first.

Walker finally nodded his assent. "You be careful." He knelt next to Joanne and gave her a hug. She hid a start but hugged him back, giving him the opportunity to drop a tiny GPS tracker into the pocket of her jacket.

Walker got up, looked around, zipped up his hoodie, followed the bouncer to the door, and walked out.

CHAPTER FOURTEEN

For the two outside, the wait was interminable. Rebecca paced, her restlessness uncontained. Broderick, just as impatient, leaned against his motorcycle in the dark, pretending not to shiver without his jacket.

"So," Broderick said after Rebecca had passed him for the twentieth time. "You and Walker?"

Rebecca stopped abruptly, her boots kicking up puffs of dust. "Why not me and Walker?"

Broderick lifted his hands, hard muscles moving. "I just asked. You have a jones for him, don't you?"

"You should talk. What about you and Joanne?"

Broderick's hands lowered, and he shrugged. "She's nice. For a human."

"That's why you're helping her? 'Cause she's so nice?"

"Hey, if it were one of my brothers missing, I'd be turning over every rock. And *my* brothers are dumb-asses. I get what she's going through."

Rebecca tamped down her anger, though her worry remained. "Yeah, I do too. If it were one of the cubs . . ."

She wouldn't be out here in a parking lot waiting to play her part. Walker had said they had to be discreet, but Shifters weren't used to being discreet, and Rebecca, in particular, was very bad at it.

She knew, however, that if she went charging in, her effort wouldn't do any good. The Shifters in the bar were un-Collared, but her Collar was plenty real and would shock the hell out of her if she tried to fight them.

She'd be outnumbered even without that disadvantage. Didn't matter that she was a Kodiak and they were puny wolves and wildcats. A group of them could drag down a bear.

"What about after Joanne finds out what's happened to Nancy?" Rebecca asked Broderick, to take her mind off things. "What are you going to do then?"

Even in the dark, she saw Broderick stiffen. "Hell if I know. Why should I do anything?"

"Give up, Brod," Rebecca said, making herself laugh. "You're smitten."

"*Smitten.* Don't make me gag. Human bullshit."

"When you're finally drooling after a mate, I'm going to rub it in so bad . . ." Rebecca trailed off, her enjoyment of teasing Broderick only so distracting. "What time is it?"

"Hell if I know. You see me wearing a sissy human watch?"

"Right, right. Lupines tell time by the light of the moon. How's that working for you? You still don't know what time it is."

Rebecca strode back to her motorcycle to the sound of

Broderick telling her what she could do with herself. She rummaged in the saddlebag until she found her cell phone and clicked it on. Just after midnight. She dropped the phone back inside, took what she needed from Walker's well-stocked duffel, and closed the saddlebag.

"Keep a lookout," she said to Broderick.

She'd already apprised him of what Walker had asked her to do. Broderick wasn't convinced it would work, but he, like Rebecca, preferred doing *something* to standing around waiting to see what happened.

Rebecca had taken three tracking devices from Walker's bag. He'd told her that while he worked on being accepted inside and dug for information, she was to choose the best vehicles to track.

She'd picked them out while she'd paced. The largest Harley in the lot, she'd decided, plus the sleek black pickup that looked innocuous but was solid and reinforced. The pickup was tricked out for off-roading—some of the unpaved roads out here were primitive.

The last one was the cute red pickup whose license plate read "SFTR GAL." Tracking a groupie might prove useful.

Rebecca moved like smoke to plant the devices. Shifter Bureau could bug Shifters without warrants, which always pissed Rebecca off, but right now she was grateful to Walker for bringing the devices. They needed to find out what these un-Collared Shifters were up to.

Rebecca had clipped the last tracker onto the wheel well of the black pickup when she saw the door to the roadhouse open. She crouched down, hiding herself, but rose again when Walker came out alone.

He kept up his slouching walk until he was well into the

shadows. Rebecca faded into deeper darkness to skirt the parking lot and join him and Broderick.

Broderick started to shout. "Where the hell is Joanne?"

"Keep it down," Rebecca snapped. "But it's a good question."

Walker, not intimidated, quickly outlined what had happened inside. Broderick stopped yelling, but he was furious. "God and Goddess, why the fuck did you leave her in there alone?"

"I couldn't extract her without endangering her," Walker said in a hard voice. "I put a tracker on her. Now we wait."

"*Wait?*" Broderick asked savagely. "I don't want to wait."

Rebecca put one hand on her hip and glared at Broderick. "Then what do you expect us to do? Charge in there, screaming? We can't take them all on. Not a boatload of un-Collared Felines and Lupines who don't think anything is wrong with breaking the leg of a Shifter barely past his Transition."

"We wait," Walker repeated firmly. "Somewhere out of sight."

"I'm not going far," Broderick said.

"We won't have to," Walker said. "But we need to get away from this place. Sooner or later, the bar will close, and there'll be a mass exodus. I doubt whatever humans own it will risk staying open after hours. If the police find out they're hiding these Shifters, they'll be in deep shit."

Rebecca said nothing, only followed Walker to her bike. Broderick rumbled something, but he stomped after them to his own motorcycle.

Walker wouldn't let them start up. They pushed the

bikes about half a mile down the road from the bar before they mounted and rode another mile or so.

They stopped in an open field, far enough from the road so that they wouldn't be seen by passing traffic—what little there was of it—but close enough to be able to follow the trackers. Walker pulled more equipment from Rebecca's saddlebag, including a tablet computer, and he set up to watch and listen.

It grew colder. Rebecca shivered. She wished she could turn bear so the chill wouldn't bother her, but she'd need to be human and nimble if they suddenly had to jump on bikes and go.

Her entire body warmed when Walker slid his arms around her from behind. His leather jacket, which he'd resumed, returning the hoodie to Broderick, held his heat.

Rebecca closed her eyes. Walker's lips found her neck, above the band of her Collar.

She envied those Shifters who'd evaded capture, living as they liked, even at the risk of going feral. She could get on her motorcycle with Walker, ride into the world, make love with him wherever they stopped, be with him forever. Cubs would come, and the cubs would learn to ride too.

But life couldn't be that simple. They had a missing woman to find, Joanne to rescue, Shifter Bureau to placate. Walker was trying to keep Rebecca out of jail for running off her restlessness in the wrong place, and Rebecca's good behavior would make sure he didn't get into trouble as well.

Walker's hands on her abdomen, his warm mouth behind her ear, was doing a pretty good job of making her forget her problems. She felt the nip of his teeth, the brush of his tongue.

I want to make love to you.

A bald statement from a man who knew how to be honest. She'd never have to guess with Walker.

A soft beeping on the tablet jerked Rebecca from her place of warmth. Walker calmly released Rebecca to pick up the tablet, as though unworried that they wouldn't pick up where they left off later.

A dot on the screen faded then reappeared a little way away from where it had vanished. "That's Joanne," Walker said. "She's leaving the bar."

Broderick shoved his face to the screen. "Where's she going?"

"Let's find out," Walker said.

Rebecca couldn't read what the machine was telling him —she didn't speak computer. Walker studied the readout for a time, made some adjustments with his fingertips, then straightened up.

"West and south. Toward Laredo."

"Then let's go," Broderick said.

"I can't monitor this while we ride. Let's wait and see where she stops."

Broderick balled his fists. "She might be dead when she stops."

"Don't worry, I won't let that happen," Walker said.

"Yeah? How the hell are you going to stop it?" Broderick grabbed Walker by the lapels of his jacket and jerked him upward. "These are Shifters in the wild. If they find out Joanne's spying, they'll kill her."

Walker didn't look one bit nervous that he hung in the grip of a powerful Shifter, but Rebecca's rage shot high.

They went on arguing, but her red anger erased the last of her control.

"She decided to risk it to find out what happened to her sister," Walker was saying. "Trust Joanne."

Broderick snorted and released him. "You wouldn't have let Rebecca stay in there."

"Rebecca can take care of herself," Walker said evenly, straightening his jacket.

"Maybe, but Joanne *can't*."

"Yes, she can," Walker said. "If she'd been too vulnerable, I'd have gotten her out somehow. She can do this."

Broderick's growls escalated. He dove at Walker again, grabbing him . . .

. . . And found a giant bear paw coming at his head. Broderick tried to duck from Rebecca's blow, but she caught him across the face. The force sent him spinning away, releasing Walker, who stumbled back a few steps before he righted himself.

Broderick came up, his Collar sparking, furious. Rebecca roared, rising on her hind legs, the Kodiak towering over both men.

How she'd become bear, Rebecca was only dimly aware. Broderick had gone for Walker, and the next thing she'd known, she was ripping off her clothes and shifting. Something ferocious had awakened in her, sending her after the threat to Walker.

The instinct, the thought deep inside Rebecca's mind whispered, *to protect the mate.*

Broderick came back at her, his fury born of the same kind of instinct.

Walker stepped between them. Crazy man—no one got

between a Lupine and a bear when they were about to go at it, but he held up his Taser, letting it crackle.

"I'll knock you both out and go on my own if you don't calm down." His voice was stern, strong, Walker in no way terrified of two beings far bigger and stronger than he was. "The signal's still moving. Give it time, and we'll go after her and extract her."

Broderick snarled his rage and frustration, but he swung away and stalked off into the darkness. Walker stood his ground, still holding the Taser.

"Becks?"

Rebecca, her heart pounding, her blood hot, made herself shift into her human form. She folded her arms across her chest once she had finished, aware that every inch of her skin was exposed.

Walker tucked away the Taser. "You all right?" he asked.

No admonishment, no staring at her in lust. Just a concerned, *You all right?*

How did he know how to melt her heart?

Rebecca shivered again. "Yeah, I'm fine," she said. "Um . . . help me find my clothes?"

Walker laughed. She rarely heard him laugh, not really. The sound was rich, full, exuding his amazing self-reliance that wrapped her and bolstered her.

He came to Rebecca, caught her around the waist, and kissed her mouth. His body was warm in the darkness, the strength in his arms keeping her upright.

Walker eased away from the kiss and smoothed a lock of her hair. "You're a wonderful woman, Becks." He let his hand linger on her cheek, the callused touch of his palm soothing. "Now, let's find your clothes."

THE SIGNAL CAME TO A STOP ABOUT TWENTY MILES west and south, where dried-up farms gave way to barren ground and oil fields. Not surprisingly, the Shifters had taken Joanne to a place far from any oil wells, where a maintenance crew might stumble across a hiding place.

"You sure this is right?" Broderick asked as they turned off engines. He scanned the darkness. "There's nothing out here."

"Yes, there is." Walker took out the tablet, brought it to life, and showed him. "There's the 35, that's where we are—there's the signal."

Rebecca's warm breath filled his ear as she leaned to look. "Good choice," she said. "You'd never know anything was here."

"Not unless you have a bag of tricks." Walker rummaged in the duffel he'd pulled out of the saddlebag and removed a set of night-vision binoculars. He peered through them for a time, made a few adjustments, and handed them to Rebecca. "Look."

Rebecca lifted the binocs to her eyes and let out a breath of surprise. Walker knew what she was seeing—several heat signatures right on top of where the signal had stopped. As he'd scanned the area, he'd seen a couple of the glows grow shorter and shorter until they'd vanished. They'd gone underground.

Rebecca lowered the binocs without a word and handed them to an impatient Broderick, who jammed them to his eyes.

"Shit," Broderick said after he'd looked for a time.

"They're *living* out here. I bet they catch rabbits and eat them raw. Ferals." He made a noise of disgust and handed the binoculars back to Walker. "Okay, so, you're right. The Shifters brought her here. Don't think they're not guarding their perimeter."

"They are." Walker had seen two hot spots wandering around away from the cluster. "Two guards it looks like. I don't think they're worried about much. This is way off the road, and if they've dug out whatever compound is down there, or built up earth walls, they'll be hard to spot from the air."

"They have to be crazy," Broderick said. "I didn't like being shoved into a Shiftertown, but this is crap. Starving in the wild was better than living in a hole."

"We don't know what's inside," Rebecca said. "Maybe they've built a luxurious palace down there."

"You're funny, Becks," Broderick answered. "Be hard to sneak in. They might have only two guards, but they'll scent us a long way off and have plenty of time to raise the alarm."

"We won't sneak in," Walker said.

Rebecca stared at him. "What, we're going to walk up and knock?"

Walker loved how she said "we." She was fully committed to the fight, not arguing about the necessity of both of them doing it. She'd only debate tactics.

"More from my bag of tricks," Walker said. "Shifters have superior senses of smell, sight, and hearing. I have things to baffle all three."

Broderick growled. "Not sure I wanted to know that."

"I stocked up for this mission," Walker said. "Flash grenades, smoke bombs, ones that make a huge stink. They'll know we're here, but we'll be in and out before they can grab us."

"Stink bombs will fuck with our senses of smell too," Broderick pointed out.

"Yes, but we'll have sight and the tracker," Walker said, holding up the tablet. "Plus, I don't need to rely on my sense of smell like you do. Stick with me, and I'll get you out again."

"He's good at this," Rebecca said to Broderick. "Trust me."

"Yeah, he's snagged your ass." Broderick looked them both over. "In more ways than one. When's the mating ceremony? Or hasn't he mate-claimed you yet?"

Instead of shooting words at Broderick in return, Rebecca became very, very quiet. She was looking at Broderick, not Walker, her eyes unreadable.

Broderick said, "Huh," and turned away, as though Rebecca had answered him.

Walker continued going through his pack, pulling out things and readying them, pretending he hadn't noticed the banter.

His skin was hot, though, his heart pumping. Mates were a serious deal with Shifters—they were joined in a mystical ceremony sacred to them, sealed by their Goddess and God. They didn't take the subject lightly.

It would be crazy to fall for Rebecca, Walker knew, but he also knew he'd moved beyond caution. He and Rebecca needed to finish this mission and then have a long, long talk.

Right now, he needed to concentrate on the immediate problem. The next half hour would be critical, and Walker couldn't jeopardize their safety and Joanne's with too much thinking about his personal life. He needed to plan, instruct Broderick and Rebecca, execute said plan, and then get the hell out of there.

He laid out all his equipment, then started telling Rebecca and Broderick what they needed to do. He spoke as though they were two soldiers under his command, not a blustering pain-in-the-ass Lupine and the Kodiak bear Shifter he was falling in love with.

"Might work," Broderick said grudgingly.

"No *might* about it," Walker said. "We make it work, because we have no choice. Right now, we retrieve Joanne. Whatever else we find out is extra."

Rebecca nodded. "You mean we focus."

"Exactly." Walker looked her straight in the eye. "One thing at a time. That way, everything important gets done."

She met his gaze, understanding in her eyes. It didn't matter that she was a Shifter, one of those beings he'd been trained to see as animals who happened to walk and talk. Rebecca was so much more, layers and layers of her that went deep down. She wasn't one woman—she was many, and Walker wanted to learn about and touch every single one of them.

Rebecca swallowed, her hair moving in the breeze that had sprung up. Clouds were forming in the sky, so much the better. A cloud passed over the moon, blotting out the light, and Rebecca nodded.

"Let's do this," she said lightly. "So we can move on to the next thing."

She and Walker shared a long look.

"Goddess," Broderick grumbled. "Now they're doing innuendo, right in front of me."

CHAPTER FIFTEEN

Rebecca found it difficult to breathe as Walker led them at a crouch to where they'd launch their attack, let alone focus. What she'd seen in his blue eyes had spoken volumes, a man ready to stop playing and get down to business—and he hadn't meant this crazy rescue.

She came after him, she and Broderick barely making a rustling in the grass. Walker's fine backside, molded by jeans, was visible to her Shifter sight, especially whenever the moon poked out from behind the clouds.

Walker made no noise at all. Rebecca and Broderick were predators, born to stalk, but Walker was silence itself.

He'd taught them his signals, and now made the one telling them to stop. "Any closer and they'll scent us," he whispered. "The wind is on our side, but who knows when it will shift?"

"You mean you don't know?" Broderick asked in the barest whisper. "I thought you knew everything."

Walker ignored him. "You're clear on what to do?" He

waited until both nodded, which he acknowledged. "On my signal."

Rebecca tensed, her muscles like too-wound springs. She sensed Broderick tensing as well. When Walker jerked his hand forward, it took everything in her not to yell as they leapt up and sprinted for the front of the compound.

Rebecca's heart pounded, her breath coming in gasps. All her life, she'd hunted and run, chasing prey or fleeing her own demons, but she'd never done anything like this. Not an all-out frontal attack. It hadn't been necessary in her old life in the wild and was forbidden in her new.

They'd almost reached the gate, which looked brand new, strong, and well oiled, when they heard a shout from the perimeter guards. Walker swung around and threw two of his scent bombs, while Rebecca yelled, "Down!" and launched a flash grenade over the gate.

White light exploded into the darkness. Rebecca had already crouched down, shielding herself, and she hoped Walker and Broderick had managed to do the same. Walker shook her after a moment, and she opened her eyes to find the guards inside the gate snarling and cursing, blinded and scent-confused.

Time for Rebecca's part. Before they'd left the motorcycles, she'd stripped down and redressed in loose T-shirt and sweatpants Walker had brought, and now she easily shucked those clothes and was bear by the time she hit the gate.

The gate was extremely strong, but no match for either a tank or a pissed off Kodiak bear. Rebecca felt the brunt of the impact, but she kept going—they needed to be inside before the Shifter guards could throw off their disorientation.

The gate's hinges screeched as they popped out of the

stone wall, then the gate clanged to the ground. One of the Shifters yelped as it struck him. Rebecca leapt over the debris and kept going.

The door to the compound wasn't as solid—probably the Shifters thought the gate with guards would be enough. Rebecca got her giant paws around the door's frame and ripped it away from the wall, then used the door as a shield as Shifters inside the compound charged out.

Walker threw another flash grenade in front of the emerging Shifters, and Broderick tossed another one plus a smoke bomb inside the compound. Rebecca squeezed her eyes shut and ducked her head behind the door just in time.

Shouting came from inside, as well as growling, and very human groaning. Poor Joanne would be caught in the blasts, but as long as the three rescuers kept their cool, they'd be able to grab her and get her out.

The scent that Rebecca caught from inside the compound, behind the stink bombs, surprisingly wasn't the fetid or disgusting smell she'd expected. The place was well aired, she discovered as she ducked inside behind Walker and Broderick, the halls lit, the hum of fans audible. They obviously had a generator somewhere.

The stairs and corridors beyond the entrance were too small for a Kodiak, so Rebecca morphed into her human form. Broderick and Walker kept on as she shifted, and she was running after them as soon as she remembered how to use two feet instead of four.

Walker was still tracking Joanne. He and Broderick kept tossing smoke and flash bombs as they needed, Rebecca trying to hold her breath as she dashed after them on bare feet.

They found Joanne on the next level down, having found a staircase that wound through the entire place. Broderick kicked in the door Walker pointed to, and Walker rolled in another flash grenade, in case Joanne was guarded. Screams and wails came from inside.

Rebecca lifted her head as soon as the flash cleared, ran inside the room, and stopped in astonishment. Instead of the dank cell she pictured, like the one in which Walker had imprisoned her, she stood in what could be a hospital room.

Two beds, one occupied, filled the space, along with machines that beeped, hummed, and ran a drip into the young Shifter lying with his leg in a hard plastic splint, not the makeshift one Walker had told her and Broderick about. The machines weren't as large and complicated as what Rebecca had seen in human hospitals, but they looked as though they got the job done.

The young man in the bed—a Lupine, not much older than Scott—had his arm over his eyes, yelling that he couldn't see. A human woman was draped over him, whimpering. She wasn't Joanne—Joanne sat in the chair next to the bed, coughing and shaking her head, her eyes jammed shut.

Broderick didn't wait. He charged in, grabbed Joanne, and hauled her up. "It's me," he said quickly when she started to fight.

Joanne clutched Broderick's jacket, unsteady on her feet. "Broderick?" She laid her head against him, sighing in relief. "Broderick."

"Two minutes," Walker said, counting down the time to exit. "We go."

Instead of leaving, though, Walker strode to the bed and

started checking the young Shifter. He did it competently, even with the young man squirming and crying out.

"Is that Tevis?" Rebecca asked. "The one you helped in the bar?"

"Yes." Walker ran his hand down Tevis's splinted leg. "He's been well cared for." He sounded as surprised as Rebecca.

"Who is that?" Tevis yelled, trying to pry open his eyes.

The human woman lifted her head, also blinking in temporary blindness. "Leave us alone!"

"It's all right," Tevis said to her. "I won't let them hurt you."

Not that Tevis was in any shape to leap from the bed and fight anyone. Even sitting up was going to give him trouble.

"I'm glad you found someone better for you," Walker told him, then he strode back out, Rebecca following.

"Wait!" Tevis shouted. "Is that you, Walter? What the fuck?"

Walker ignored him, making the signal for the others to follow him again. "One minute, thirty."

"No, not yet," Joanne said, still clinging to Broderick. "Nancy's here. We can't go without her."

Walker snapped around. "What? Where?"

"Two doors down. I saw her, but they wouldn't let me out of Tevis's room."

"Two doors which way?"

Joanne tried to look around, eyes screwed up, but she clearly still couldn't see. "To the left."

Walker was already moving, Broderick and Joanne behind him. Rebecca paused long enough to grab a sweat jacket, probably Tevis's, and shrug it on.

The door two down from Tevis's was locked, but Broderick easily kicked it in. These doors hadn't been reinforced to withstand Shifters.

They found another hospital room inside, this one with one bed and more machines. Walker didn't bother with a flash grenade this time, but the Shifter man in the bed—Feline by the look of him—was gray-faced and only groaned when he saw them dash in.

The woman sitting by the Shifter's bedside, her hand firmly locked around the Feline's broad one, looked around in shock, then sprang to her feet.

"Jo-Jo?"

"Nance." Joanne began to cry, rushing forward to her sister. "Oh, Nance I've been so scared for you."

Nancy pulled away as Joanne tried to hug her. Rebecca noted that the Shifter in the bed hadn't released her hand.

"Jo-Jo, what are you doing here?" Nancy asked, her voice cracking. "How did you find me?" She peered fearfully at Walker, Broderick, and Rebecca.

"These are friends," Joanne said quickly. "It's all right. They'll get you home."

"Forty-five seconds," Walker said.

"Let's go," Rebecca said. "Run away now, have reunion later."

Nancy jerked away from Joanne. "No. I can't leave him."

"Yes, you can," Joanne said, reaching for her again. "I came here with a hurt Shifter, but they already found another woman to take care of him. I get it—Shifters need physical contact to heal. They'll bring in someone else for him."

"No, *you* don't get it." Nancy again broke away, never

loosening the ill Shifter's hand. "This is Aleck. He needs me."

"Thirty seconds," Walker said.

Broderick growled. "Joanne, we need to go."

"Nance," Joanne implored.

Nancy shook her head. She looked much like Joanne, though her hair was a shade darker. Her hair was clean and brushed, shining in the lamplight. She'd been able to bathe, apparently, and her clothes, a tight sweater and skirt, were likewise clean, as were her glitter-studded red sneakers.

"Twenty seconds," Walker said, his tone sharper.

"Would you stop doing that?" Broderick snapped.

"No." Walker's mouth was a grim line. "Broderick, take Joanne out. Now. No more time."

Broderick didn't argue. He walked forward, seized Joanne, and firmly turned her around with him. She protested, and Nancy looked worried but stayed in place.

"They'll do what they need to," Broderick said to Joanne as he propelled her out the door. "Walker might be human, but he's trained for this."

Broderick didn't stop as he talked. His voice faded as he took Joanne down the hall.

"My mission is to find you and get you home," Walker said to Nancy. "That's what I'm doing, with or without your cooperation."

Nancy's eyes widened, and she backed to the bed. Aleck, who'd not said a word during the encounter, finally lifted his head.

"Mine," he said clearly.

"She's human," Walker told him. "You're a Collarless Shifter. You don't own anyone."

Rebecca clutched the edges of the jacket she'd taken and moved to Walker's side. Aleck wasn't clamping down on Nancy's hand to keep her from running away—they were clinging to each other. Terrified of being torn apart.

Aleck wore no Collar at all, not even a fake one, but his color wasn't good. He was suffering from something, though Rebecca had no idea what. Shifters didn't get sick. Hurt, yes, and occasionally there was a malady that could kill them, but that occurrence was rare.

Aleck's scent wasn't quite right for a Feline. Not that Rebecca knew much about Felines, despite being neighbors with them for the last twenty years.

"What's wrong with him?" Rebecca asked Nancy.

At the same moment, Walker said, "Time." Meaning they were out of it.

Another voice sounded at the door. "He's starting to go feral," a male Shifter said. "That's what's wrong with him. But I'm not going to let that happen."

"Shit," Walker whispered.

They'd planned several contingencies for their exit strategy, including what happened if they were trapped by the compound's Shifters. Rebecca ripped off the jacket, let her bear fill the room, and ran straight at the open door and the Shifter standing there.

The next moment she found herself looking down the rune-covered blade of a Sword of the Guardian, its tip nestled right against her heart.

CHAPTER SIXTEEN

For a few moments, Walker couldn't see anything beyond the bulk of bear until Rebecca slowly, slowly became a human woman again. The lush flesh of her back and buttocks beckoned his eye, and Walker had a hell of a time taking his gaze from them to assess the situation.

A Shifter in human form stood in the corridor, the point of the huge sword in his hand touching Rebecca's chest, right between her breasts. The tip brushed her skin but didn't break it.

Feline, Walker's thoughts went. *No Collar. Blue eyes. Guardian? Or did he steal the sword?*

"Who are you?" Walker asked.

"You're in *my* house," the Feline answered, never taking his gaze, or the sword, from Rebecca. "My territory. Who are *you?*"

For the first time tonight, Walker didn't have a ready answer. He'd come up with plans for most circumstances, but not for meeting what looked like a Guardian with no Collar in an underground compound in the middle of South Texas.

Guardians weren't leaders. Granted, they were high in the pecking order, but they took orders from the leader of their pride, pack, or clan. They served to not only send Shifters to the Summerland, but to fight at the leader's side and protect the weaker members of the community.

In the Austin Shiftertown, the Guardian, Sean, was also a tracker, meaning he investigated problems and generally kept an eye on things both within and without Shiftertown. He was also the leader's younger brother.

Guardians were chosen by the Goddess—apparently—in a mystical ceremony on the occasion of the previous Guardian's death. The new Guardian immediately took up his sword and sent the former Guardian to dust.

"Who's leader here?" Walker asked, Rebecca remaining mute.

The Feline shook his head. "You're out of your depth, human. Who are *you*, Ursine?" The tip of the sword moved a little, making the barest scratch on Rebecca's skin. "Not many Kodiaks around here. You must be from the Austin Shiftertown. The Kodiak there is Ronan. That means you're the female called Rebecca, who lives with him but is not his mate. Ronan's mate is a human, and you've taken in cubs not your own to raise."

Rebecca's chest lifted with her breath, her face tightening as the Guardian rattled off his perfect guesses. "I didn't know they let Shifters without Collars access the Guardian Network," she said, keeping her voice light.

"The Guardian Network has nothing to do with Collars," the Feline said. His eyes were a strange shade of blue, one Walker had never seen before on a Shifter. Light, clear, but at the same time possessing a dark intensity. "Guardians and the Network existed long before the humans discovered Shifters. Now, tell me why you've broken into my compound."

"To rescue the people you kidnapped," Rebecca said steadily, while Walker waited, ready to attack. "What did you think?"

The Feline's expression didn't change. He had interesting hair as well—it was buzzed short and very light blond but crossed with soot-black streaks. "No one here is kidnapped," he said. "They come because they want to be here."

"Oh, right, one big happy family," Rebecca said. "You forced a groupie here—several of them, in fact—so they could hold Shifters' hands and help them heal. The one who came with Tevis of the broken leg wasn't here by choice."

"No, she wanted to come. Begged to, from what I was told." The Guardian sounded unimpressed, his sword never wavering. "They all do. They're looking for what they can't find in the human world—people who need them and take care of them."

"Which you provide, of course," Rebecca said. "And if they want to leave, you let them go?"

"Yes." His eyes were rock steady, his mouth in a flat line.

"Good," Walker said, hand on the Taser in his jacket pocket. "Then we'll take Nancy and be gone."

The Guardian's voice hardened. "Nancy stays."

"Does she want to?" Walker asked. "Or did you make her think she wants to?"

Anger flickered across his face. "If you take Aleck's mate from him, he'll deteriorate and die, and I'll have to send him to dust. She's keeping him alive."

"His mate?" Walker wasn't that surprised, given how Aleck and Nancy had held on to each other. He'd seen Ronan and Elizabeth do that; Tiger and Carly as well.

Nancy answered, her voice faint but resolute. "He mated us, Sun and Moon. I'm not leaving Aleck. Tell Jo-Jo I'm sorry."

"Fair enough," Walker said. "But you might have called your sister and told her. Saved us all a lot of trouble."

"No calls," the Guardian said, taking back the conversation. "No phones work here. No contact with the outside world."

Of course not. Contact from here meant risk of exposure. Going to the roadhouse also meant risk, but the Shifters would have to somehow find mates to breed cubs. Walker had seen very few female Shifters at the roadhouse, and likely not many more lived here. The disproportion of males to females had been even greater in the wild.

Once these Shifters convinced a groupie to come here, Walker reflected, if she stayed and disappeared from the world, well, she was only a groupie. As had happened with Nancy, the police wouldn't be in a hurry to look for a woman who probably had simply holed up with a Shifter.

But Walker and Rebecca weren't groupies—Walker was from Shifter Bureau, and Rebecca was a powerful Shifter from a powerful Shiftertown. This Guardian couldn't afford to let them go, which meant that Walker and Rebecca were in deep shit. Broderick *might* have made it out—they'd know eventually.

Walker had been trained to fight, not negotiate, but he'd learned in the big, bad world that sometimes words could save a lot of bloodshed and unnecessary death.

"Can you tell us your name?" he asked. "Easier to talk about my fate if I can say a name."

"I don't know yours," the Guardian said. He cast a disparaging look at what was left of Walker's face makeup. "And that groupie shit isn't going to fly. Who are you?"

"Walker Danielson. Major, US Army." Walker paused after he snapped this off. "Friend to Shifters."

"You must be." The Guardian returned his stern blue gaze to Rebecca. "She's not afraid of you. In fact, she's drawn to you. You're a pair."

Rebecca's cheeks grew red. "Hey, now, that's none of your business."

"I regret the circumstances," the Guardian said, his tone unchanged. "You should be mated. But I can't let you go."

A promise to never tell anyone about him and his compound would be laughed at. Neither Walker nor Rebecca could keep such a secret, and the Guardian knew it. Broderick certainly wouldn't.

"You're compromised," Walker told him. "Accept it, and bug out. By the time I can rain hell down upon here, you could be long gone."

The Guardian flicked a glance at Walker that was almost amused, but his sword remained at Rebecca's chest. "I like it here. It took me a long time to build this refuge."

"How are you not feral?" Rebecca asked him. "The un-Collared Shifters that were found in Mexico went feral—

they sequestered females, kept cubs locked in a basement. Disgusting stuff."

The Guardian's voice was rich and full. "If you're referring to the feral who calls himself Miguel—he was born Scottish. He was an idiot, and I hope he's either dead or about to be. He wanted to live wild, as though he hadn't had an apartment in Glasgow before Shifters were exposed. I want Shifters to stay in the wild too, but that's no reason to live in our own excrement."

"You have pretty good tech," Walker said, glancing at the equipment around Aleck.

"We do," the Guardian said impatiently. "Stop trying to condescend to me, Major. You suck at it."

That was true. The Guardian wasn't a Shifter desperate and beaten, ready to go out fighting. He was an alpha, had a clear grasp of each scenario that could happen from here on out, and had no qualms about killing Walker and Rebecca to keep himself and this compound safe.

"No matter what you do, you'll have to move from this place," Walker said. "If Rebecca and I go missing, there will be a hunt."

"I know that. Also for the other Shifter and his girlfriend my men have already caught on the perimeter. Your Shifter friends will find your bodies, many miles from here. Rebecca and the Lupine will be the victims of Shifter hunters. Humans sometimes get caught in the crossfire."

True, if they were found far enough away, and these Shifters covered their tracks well, no one would trace them back here.

"So, that's our choice?" Rebecca asked. "Die or move in?"

"You'd never leave your clan and cubs," the Guardian said. "The pull to them would overwhelm you, in the end. Even your mate couldn't keep you here."

"I don't know," Rebecca said, making a careful shrug. "I'm something of a loner."

The Guardian gave a short laugh. "No, you're not. Bears live far apart in the wild, true, but they don't cut off *all* contact. And you've been changed by captivity. Being with others sustains you. You've learned how to love, and you can't be ripped away from that now. I know this, because it's what happened to me."

His voice went somber, his eyes seeming darker, or maybe that was a trick of the light.

"In that case," Walker broke in. "Turn yourself in, take the Collar, stay with your people."

More laughter, but that didn't mean his hand softened on the sword. "Screw you. You still don't get it, human. This place is proof that Shifters don't need Collars or containment to keep from turning violent or going feral. We just need each other."

"Nice," Walker said. "What about him?" He jerked his thumb at Aleck.

The Guardian shrugged. "It happens. But he's going to pull through, I swear to the Goddess."

"You still haven't told us your name," Rebecca pointed out.

"That's because we're not going to link arms and sing 'Kumbaya,'" the Guardian said impatiently. "I'm going to kill you."

"And send me to dust?"

"Not for me to do it. When your bodies are found, your own Guardian will perform that task."

"That's a risk," Rebecca said quickly. "If the human police find us first, they might not let him. You'd have my soul and Broderick's stuck here, instead of being released to the Summerland?"

Smart argument. Guardians felt a keen responsibility to make sure no Shifter soul was trapped to its body or left to wander aimlessly on this plane of existence. Though Shifters had no formal organization for their religion and had never built the equivalent of a church or temple, Shifters had more sense of and devotion to their spiritual beliefs than many humans Walker knew.

"Fine," the Guardian said. "I'll dust you myself. My name's Kendrick. Pleased to meet you." And he drove the sword straight at Rebecca's heart.

REBECCA HIT THE GROUND. SHE WASN'T TRAINED IN combat fighting, but she'd sparred plenty with Ronan, and she'd learned how to fight dirty. She spun on the floor and aimed a hard kick at Kendrick's balls.

He was Feline, though, which meant he was much faster than a bear could ever be. He'd sprung away and was halfway down the corridor, heading deeper into the compound, before Rebecca's foot connected with the space he'd been in.

Walker leapt over Rebecca, his Taser out, and dropped a Shifter who'd come running to aid Kendrick. That Shifter went down, but a second Shifter smacked the Taser out of Walker's hand.

Walker spun away from him, reached down, and pulled Rebecca to her feet. Then the crazy man, instead of trying to run for it, went after the Guardian.

Kendrick hadn't gone far. He turned back at the end of the passage and faced them without fear, his sword ready. His Shifters bottled in Rebecca and Walker from behind, blocking the way out.

"Terrific!" Rebecca yelled at Walker as she took up a fighting stance. "Got any more tricks in that bag of yours? Another flash grenade? Smoke bomb? Tear gas? A tranq rifle? Six pissed-off Shifter trackers?"

"Just one thing," Walker said, sounding way too calm. He held a device in his hand, too small to be a weapon. It looked like a tiny black box with a button on it. He showed it to Kendrick, lifted the device over his head, and firmly thumbed the button.

Rebecca ducked, hands over her head, waiting for the worst. The other Shifters, except Kendrick, ducked with her.

Nothing happened. No explosion, no flash, no nets falling on top of their captors. Just silence and one of Kendrick's Shifters breaking into nervous laughter.

Kendrick attacked. His sword flashed, lightning fast, at Walker's neck. Walker couldn't move quickly enough. The blade contacted and drew blood, lots of it. Walker fell.

"No!" Rebecca sprinted toward them. Halfway there, she shifted to bear, charging Kendrick as a roaring, raging Kodiak. She was fast enough this time to impact Kendrick. He crashed into the wall, losing hold of his sword, which clanged to the floor.

The Guardian pushed himself upright, no longer human. His clothes ripped, falling away, until a giant white tiger emerged from the cocoon of them to face Rebecca.

Rebecca stopped for a heartbeat of amazement. The only tiger Shifter she was aware of was Tiger, a Bengal, who had been bred in a lab. She'd never heard of any other tiger Shifter, let alone a white one.

The hesitation gave Kendrick the advantage. He came at Rebecca with claw-spiked paws that were Feline fast. Rebecca was about half again Kendrick's size, but Felines had the benefit of speed and ferocity.

Rebecca fought hard, but Kendrick got in three blows to her one. Her fur turned away some of his attack, but his claws started to dig deep, and pain began as blood flowed. Rebecca's Collar was sparking at the same time, trying to stop her, biting agony into every nerve.

In her rage, Rebecca barely felt it. She had to fight to protect Walker. To get him out of here. He was too vulnerable, unable to physically face Shifters, especially ones without controlling Collars.

Protect him! her instincts screamed at her. *Guard the mate!*

Females whose mates were threatened were the most dangerous Shifters of all.

Somewhere at the bottom of her mind, the human Rebecca was thinking, in shock, *Mate?*

She's drawn to you, Kendrick had said. *You're a pair.* Broderick had made a similar observation.

Rebecca the bear knew exactly what Walker was. Had known since he'd been dumped, wrapped in duct tape, on her living room floor. She'd looked into ice-blue eyes that had been full of irritation, and had fallen hard.

And now Walker might die because of her. He'd been sent out to complete a mission that the police and Shifter Bureau should have, because Rebecca had been arrested. She knew that the only reason she'd been set free was because Walker had struck a deal with the bureau. He'd convinced his superiors that having Rebecca help him would be more efficient use of resources than executing her.

She wouldn't have put Walker in that position at all if she'd been more careful. Rebecca had known she should stay away from parts of the airport that were now in private hands, but she'd been too arrogant to bother paying attention.

For that, Walker would be killed by these Shifters in this unknown compound ruled over by a crazed white tiger Guardian.

Rebecca roared, fury pouring out of her. She struck and struck at the tiger, claws contacting, teeth ripping. Her Collar sparked insanely, but she pushed aside the pain to fight on.

Walker, instead of curling into a ball and protecting himself or trying to run the hell out of there, was fighting with her. He gave the other Shifters trying to get to Rebecca respectable punches and kicks, keeping them off her back while she fought the whirlwind of the Guardian.

Kendrick's eyes were dark blue now, wide and filled with terrible anger, his ears flat on his head as he fought. He was a beautiful animal—or would be if he weren't trying so hard to disembowel Rebecca and rip out her throat.

And he might succeed. Rebecca feared she'd stumble at

the wrong time, and then he'd be on her. A smaller animal could bring down a larger by being fast and tricky.

Rebecca caught glimpses of Walker, a flurry of fighting man, ducking the wolves and Felines going for him, getting in plenty of blows before they could touch him with teeth or claws.

She saw him bend down and retrieve his Taser, zapping another Shifter with it. That Shifter yelled and fell, but another quickly took his place.

"Shit, are you two still down here?" Broderick's voice boomed from behind them. "Damn." He was fighting Shifters as well, no sign of Joanne.

Rebecca and the Guardian battled on. She knew she'd lose eventually. Kendrick was strong, and this was his home. Who knew, but he might have a mate, cubs, in the compound behind him, and be fighting like mad to protect them.

The fear of losing galvanized Rebecca. She had to at least get Walker out. She would clear a path for him and Broderick, and cover their escape. Rebecca might not make it, but at least her mate would survive.

Walker's Taser went flying again. This time, the hand that picked it up was Nancy's. She stood in the middle of the corridor, looking desperate, and zapped the first Shifter she could. Broderick.

He shouted and then hit the floor with a crash. Walker went for Nancy.

"No!" Nancy screamed. "You leave my mate alone!"

Another zap. Rebecca's heart nearly burst as she saw Walker fall facedown, Shifters surrounding him.

The white tiger's claws came at her. At the same time,

the fire of many volts crashed into her side, combining with the Collar's stinging shocks.

The floor seemed to come up at her, Rebecca's weight sending her down fast. She managed to take a wolf Shifter with her, he groaning as his head smacked cement.

Females whose mates are threatened, Rebecca thought as Nancy's glittery sneakers came to rest next to her nose. *The most dangerous of us all.*

And then, nothing.

CHAPTER SEVENTEEN

The silken weight of Rebecca's hair moved against Walker's bare arm as she stirred. Walker smoothed it back as best he could with cuffs around his thick wrists.

Rebecca opened her eyes—sweet brown eyes that held the sultriness of a woman who'd just woken up with her lover. "Hey," she said.

"Hey." Walker stroked her hair again. "Welcome back."

"Mmm. I like this dream."

Walker didn't answer. He knew exactly what their odds were for survival, and he saw no reason to bring down the mood by talking about them.

Rebecca lay with her head in his lap, her body curled up next to his. Walker had laid his leather jacket over her, and her firm legs peeked from under it, her round hip rising in a sensual curve. A beautiful, beautiful woman, never mind she was covered with scratches, bite marks, and dried blood. Walker was pretty beat up himself.

Rebecca murmured again, burrowing into his lap. Walker liked that she did so without constraint, without shyness. She wanted to be here, with him, her head massaging parts of him that didn't care what danger they were in.

They were locked inside a five-by-five cell, which was empty, apart from them. No windows, a heavy, bolted wooden door, a light bulb, a floor. Nothing else.

Rebecca opened her eyes again, blinking, long black lashes brushing her skin. Her brow furrowed as her full awareness returned. "Where the hell are we?"

"In a cell in Kendrick's compound."

"Aw, shit." Rebecca pushed herself up, her hand going to her head. The cuffs they'd fixed around her wrists clanked. "Broderick?"

"They got him. I saw them push him into another room."

"What about Kendrick's plan to kill us and dump our bodies a long way from here?"

Walker shrugged. "I put a dent in their plans."

Rebecca sat up straight, tucking her legs under her. She glanced at her naked body and blushed, closing Walker's jacket around her more securely.

"What dent?"

"The last thing in my bag of tricks."

Rebecca leaned against the wall next to him, her eyes narrowing. She had plenty of smarts, this bear Shifter. Rebecca would never be a helpless woman.

"Are you going to tell me?" she asked. "What did that thing you clicked do? Blow up the outer walls?"

"No. Triggered a remote that Broderick took outside

with him. A signal from in here wouldn't carry far, but far enough to the tracker Broderick tossed into the dirt when he ran out with Joanne. *That* tracker is broadcasting a distress signal and the exact location of this compound."

"Who to?"

The door scraped open. Kendrick stood in the doorway, restored to clothes, his ice-blue eyes crystal sharp. His neck and face held abrasions from Rebecca's teeth and claws, but otherwise, he looked unscathed.

The two bouncers from the roadhouse stood behind him. Not that Walker and Rebecca, exhausted and in cuffs, were in any shape to try to rush past them.

"A good question," Kendrick said. "We found your tracking device. It's not broadcasting anymore."

The Feline bouncer, the one who'd first answered the door at the club, smiled, showing all his teeth. Walker guessed he'd enjoyed himself stomping the life out of the device.

"Who did you summon?" Kendrick asked. "Police? I have the county sheriff in my pocket. He doesn't even realize I'm a Shifter."

"What about Shifter Bureau?" Rebecca demanded. "You have *them* in your pocket?"

Kendrick's eyes flickered. "What self-respecting Shifter and her man-whore would summon Shifter Bureau? Even if that man-whore works for them? Shifter Bureau would stick *her* in a cage the same as they would us. They arrest first, ask questions later."

"I know that," Walker said. "So, no, not Shifter Bureau."

"Then who?" Kendrick asked, but offhandedly, as though he had only a passing interest.

"Dylan Morrissey."

Silence. Kendrick's gaze locked to Walker, rage igniting in his eyes. Walker had no doubt that, with Kendrick's access to the Guardian Network, he'd damn well know all about Dylan.

Kendrick moved across the room in Feline swiftness and yanked Walker up by his shirt. "You summoned *Dylan*?"

"Yep," Walker said, meeting his gaze without fear. "Strictly speaking, this is his territory."

"No," Kendrick said. He eased his grip from Walker, leaving Walker on his feet. "It's mine."

"Dylan used to be the Austin Shiftertown leader," Walker said in a reasonable tone. "Before he stepped down and gave the job to his son. When the San Antonio leader died, Dylan manipulated the next one into place. That Shifter answers to Dylan, no matter what the humans think. Dylan controls almost all of central and South Texas. He'll know the exact borders."

From the look on Kendrick's face, he already knew this. He'd been hiding out in this compound not only from the human authorities, but from Dylan. Liam might be leader of the Austin Shiftertown now, and another Shifter might lead San Antonio's, but Dylan still wielded huge amounts of power. He was Liam's mentor and top tracker, and was very good at pulling strings behind the scenes.

Kendrick grabbed Walker again, jerking him close. Rebecca clawed her way up the wall to her feet, giving a warning growl, but Walker gazed fearlessly back at Kendrick.

Kendrick's blue eyes held not only anger but something

else, a worry that went beyond normal fear. He shook Walker, his voice becoming a deep, tiger snarl.

"You fucking idiot. You've ruined everything . . ."

Before Walker could speak or Rebecca could grab for Kendrick, Kendrick tossed Walker away, spun, and ran past his startled bodyguards and out of the room.

———

REBECCA WAS TORN BETWEEN HURTLING AFTER Kendrick and making sure Walker, who'd hit the wall and fallen back to the ground, was all right.

She needn't have worried. Walker was on his feet faster than the other Shifters could react, his cuffs coming apart and clanking to the floor. *He's a master escape artist, remember?* she told herself.

"Come on, sweetheart," Walker said.

He pulled Rebecca along with him, her hands still cuffed in front of her, but that didn't slow her down as she helped Walker fight off the bouncers. The two Shifters were tough and angry, but also uncertain. Whatever Kendrick had gone to do, they didn't know.

Walker punched and kicked, ducking the larger men's blows and proving himself even faster than the Feline. Rebecca didn't have time to stand back and admire Walker's hand-to-hand techniques, but he had skill enough to get them past the Shifters and into the corridor.

Once through the narrow door, Rebecca shifted to bear, which let her easily break the handcuffs. The cuffs had, in fact, been made to hold Shifters—but there were Shifters, and then there were the largest bear Shifters on the planet.

Walker should have run for the entrance. Instead, he started in the other direction, as before, following Kendrick.

Rebecca snarled and went after him. It wasn't easy to run in the narrow corridors, but she was faster as bear, and shifting back would take precious time.

She scrambled around a tight corner to see Walker grab a door Kendrick had just gone through, yank it open, and run in after him.

Rebecca reached the open doorway and came to a staggering halt. Kendrick had barreled into a room that was as blank as the cell she and Walker had been locked in, only three times bigger, and this one had someone inside it.

Three someones, all very small.

"Dad!" the one who looked to be about nine or ten yelled as Kendrick turned and faced Walker.

The other two were in animal form—two small, blue-eyed white tigers yowling in terror.

Rebecca froze. Walker came to a halt, his hands lifting.

Kendrick had retrieved his sword. He unsheathed it and pointed it straight at Walker, at the same time pushing the cubs behind him.

"Easy," Walker said. "We won't hurt them."

"No," Kendrick said clearly. "You won't."

He had a remote switch, like the one Walker had used. Rebecca scented something odd, looked up, then plunged into the room, seized Walker between her paws, and dragged him rapidly back out.

Kendrick clicked the remote. Instead of the silence that had followed Walker's switch, a roar filled the air, followed by several tons of rock and dust falling from the ceiling.

The Shifters that had followed Walker and Rebecca

shouted and scrambled away, running for safety. Rebecca was already moving, but the cascade from the bursting cell caught Walker, ripping him from Rebecca's grip, knocking him to the ground, and pouring masonry, concrete, and rebar directly on top of him.

CHAPTER EIGHTEEN

The rumbling continued, but Rebecca stood stunned as dust and rock rained down around her. A huge wall of rubble blocked what had been the windowless room Kendrick had been in, and Walker's body was hidden in all that mess.

Rebecca let out a roar that threatened to bring down the rest of the building and started digging with bear paws, throwing aside chunks of concrete no man would be able to lift. Underneath this crushing pile was her mate.

Dead? Alive? But how could he be under there and still be alive?

Rebecca raged and wept inside as she dug. She loved Walker but had kept her distance from him all these months, telling herself she wanted to sort out her feelings.

The truth was she'd been afraid of letting herself get close to him, afraid of facing pain if Walker decided he didn't want a large, sassy-mouthed woman who could turn into a bear around him on a day-to-day basis. She'd been afraid to love, afraid of what it would do to her.

Walker had never been afraid of *her*. He'd looked her in the eye, given her his wry smile, and told her that he wanted her. And now he might be dead, and Rebecca would have wasted every bit of time she could have had with him second-guessing herself.

There would never be another Walker Danielson. When he was gone, it would be forever.

Rebecca kept digging, oblivious to everything but finding Walker. She could barely breathe from all the dust, and her lungs begged for air. Something was wrong with one of her legs—it kept bending when she didn't tell it to, and it hurt like hell.

She'd deal with all that later. For now, she needed to save her mate.

The rubble came away, but more fell from the ceiling at the same time. The compound was in chaos. Rebecca heard screaming, cursing, running, fighting. Broderick's voice booming. Nancy wailing from down the hall. Had Aleck been hurt? Killed? What about the young kid, Tevis?

That was all in the background, beyond Rebecca's immediate focus. Her entire attention at the moment was on saving Walker.

She threw aside another chunk of concrete and nearly wept when she saw a black T-shirt and dusty jeans among the gray rocks. Rebecca lifted away a piece of ceiling that had tented around him, saving him from being crushed, but Walker didn't move. He lay facedown and silent, his body covered in contusions and filth, his hair coated with blood.

Bears could be incredibly gentle when they had to be.

Rebecca hooked claws into the fabric of Walker's shirt without touching his skin, and turned him over.

His face was gray, his shirt covered with blood. Rebecca bent down to him, terrified he was dead, and then she saw his chest rise with a ragged breath.

Relief staggered her, but he wasn't safe yet. Footsteps pounded behind her, and Rebecca roared, stepping protectively over Walker.

The Shifters were all running away though. The compound was compromised, and they knew it.

Their fleeing wasn't as chaotic as she'd first thought. The Shifters were getting the hell out of there, but in an orderly fashion, as though following a plan. Even Kendrick blowing up this part of the compound had likely been part of an escape scenario.

Walker opened his eyes. Not all the way—Rebecca saw the gleam of blue between his lids. He groaned.

Rebecca shook him. She didn't have time to shift back to human to make him understand; she'd only get him out safely as her bear.

She planted her massive paw on his chest and moved him back and forth until Walker took a deeper breath, and said, "What?"

Rebecca crouched down, lower, lower. Pain spiked through her leg, but she forced herself to ignore it. Walker stared at her uncomprehendingly for a moment, then he hauled himself up, bracing himself on Rebecca's shoulder as he forced himself to his feet.

He half climbed, half fell onto her back, locked his fingers into her fur, and said in a dust-clogged voice, "Okay, I'm good."

Rebecca rose and ran straight down the corridor, never minding what she ran over or shoved out of her way.

Broderick was ahead of her, carrying a screaming Nancy over his shoulder. Rebecca worried for Aleck and Tevis, but Broderick was right to take Nancy out. This place wouldn't last much longer. Kendrick had triggered some massive destruction.

Up the stairs and through the broken front door, the stench of the smoke bombs lingering. On past the gate that still lay on the ground, out through the opening and into the night. Joanne waited outside the gates, huddled into Broderick's hoodie, and started crying when she saw Nancy.

Joanne started forward to gather in her sister, but the moment Nancy's feet touched the ground, she tried to run back inside. Rebecca blocked Nancy's way, and Broderick seized her again.

"We'll get him out," Broderick shouted at Nancy. "We have help. He'll be safe."

Rebecca ran on again into the cold darkness, putting as much distance between herself and the compound as she could. By the time Walker said, "We're clear," Rebecca had already slowed. She took a few more stumbling steps before she fell, first to her front legs, and then flat on her belly.

Walker rolled off her. "Becks." He put his hands on her head, turning her bear face up to him. "Becks—sweetheart—you all right?"

Rebecca wanted to lie there forever, half insensible in the dust, with Walker stroking her head and calling her *sweetheart* in a broken voice. It was so comfortable on the ground, the dirt soft. Her mate was with her, alive, and she totally needed a nap . . .

She felt herself passing out. The pain from fighting and her Collar going off was catching up to her, as well as whatever she'd done to her right leg. Her body was trying to plunge her into unconsciousness to keep her from the agony.

Before darkness could take over, she shifted back to human. It hurt—oh, crap, it hurt—but she ended up in her naked human form, her head cradled on Walker's lap.

"Becks." Walker bent over her, his lips touching her face, her mouth. He ran his hands down her body—checking for injury, she knew, as he was trained to do.

His touches were caressing, soothing, lending her strength. *The touch of a mate.* He was healing her. Rebecca let her hands rest on his thighs, turned her head to press a kiss to his rock-hard stomach. She was his mate. They'd heal each other.

A lot of Shifters seemed to be running around. Rebecca didn't have to lift her head to catch the scents, the sounds of familiar voices.

They'd all come—the Morrissey men, and the trackers, including Spike, Ellison with his deep Texas drawl, the comforting bass rumble of Ronan.

One of the Shifters came to tower over her and Walker. Rebecca looked up to see Tiger gazing a long way down at them from his tawny eyes, the orange stripes in his black hair highlighted by moonlight.

Tiger took in Walker and Rebecca in silence for a moment, then gave one firm nod. "Good," he said, and walked away.

Ronan was there, going down on one knee beside Rebecca. He touched Rebecca's hair and sighed in relief.

"Scared us when we saw the explosion. I always knew you were tough, Becks, but shit."

Rebecca snuggled against Walker. Ronan laid a jacket over her—Walker's leather one again, which someone must have picked up on the way out of the compound. The jacket held Walker's scent, and Rebecca closed her eyes to enjoy it.

"About time you got here," she murmured to Ronan.

"Huh," Ronan grunted, but he sounded amused. "Thank *this* guy for calling the cavalry."

Ronan walked away, his voice blending in with the other Shifters'.

"Thank you," Rebecca whispered to Walker. There was more she wanted to say—so much more—but nothing would come out.

"Shh," Walker said, stroking her hair. "You rest now, and I'll make you better."

Sounded good to her. To the touch of her mate's hand, Rebecca let the sounds of the night slide together, pain floating away on the happiness of the moment.

———

KENDRICK FOLLOWED HIS ESCAPE PLAN TO THE LETTER. Knock out the wall between the enemy and the cubs, flee with them down the tunnel that opened from a hidden door in the safe room.

He ran down the dark passage, the silence within telling him he wasn't being followed. The two smallest cubs, still in tiger form, clung to his shoulders, while Robbie ran along beside him on human feet. He was too old to be carried,

Robbie would declare. It was true that the cub—not Kendrick's; he was a Lupine—was already a good little runner.

The tunnel went for three miles, emerging into an empty field under the night sky. Kendrick unlocked the gate at its end and pushed the Harley that waited there out into quiet darkness.

The cubs all went into specially modified saddle bags, helmets on their heads. Kendrick straddled the bike, the Sword of the Guardian in its sheath on his back, and started up.

The Shifters from the compound would regroup at the rendezvous point and begin again. Kendrick's trackers would take care of the sick and injured, and bring any who didn't make it to Kendrick to be sent to dust.

Kendrick's job was to get the three cubs—the only wee ones they had—to safety. The two youngest were his; Robbie had been rescued when his wolf Shifter parents had been killed.

Kendrick's Shifters had started over twice now—perhaps the Goddess would smile upon them the third time.

The cubs were silent, scared, and Kendrick didn't blame them. They'd been tiny when they'd moved here, and the compound in Texas dry lands was the only home they knew. The compound had been an abandoned and forgotten military bunker from World War II, dug out and fortified by the Shifters a few years ago. All their hard work was now dust.

Kendrick had thought this area remote enough to be safe, but apparently, he'd been wrong. After the San Antonio leader had been ousted and killed a couple years ago, there had been no activity out here, and he'd assumed they'd be left in peace. He knew all about Dylan Morrissey but had, until now, successfully eluded that Shifter's detection.

Dylan and his sons were good at rounding up un-Collared Shifters and bringing them in, under their control. Kendrick didn't want that for his cubs—for any of his Shifters. He wanted them to be free, forever.

Alaska would be their next destination. In the vast wilderness near the Pacific, in the fjords and mountains, they'd make another home.

Kendrick rode for miles, on through Texas darkness, down a highway that few traveled, especially this late at night. They flowed past old farmland, through dry washes, and around oil fields with their clanking pumps moving up and down like bizarre grazing beasts.

He rode until the motorcycle needed fuel. The boys would need to eat, as well, and use the bathroom. Boys ate a lot, nonstop if they could, his mate had said the last time he'd seen her.

Kendrick pushed the deep pain of losing her aside as he sought a gas station. He'd rolled into the outskirts of Laredo, a town large enough to have places open this late, small enough that people here had probably never seen a Shifter and wouldn't recognize one if they did.

He pulled into a gas station and climbed stiffly from the bike. The fight with the bear had been tough. She'd been protecting her mate, and her ferocity had been intense. It would be a while before Kendrick threw off the soreness from that battle.

He'd have to leave the sword with the bike if he wanted

to take the little ones into the gas station's convenience store. The clerk would only call the police if he saw a tall man stride inside with a giant sword strapped to his back.

Kendrick wrapped the sword in a thin tarp and stowed it on the rack on the bike he'd made for just this purpose, then filled the tank.

No way would he leave anything as precious as the cubs out here though. The wee ones had already shifted and dressed, and Robbie was bouncing on his toes, growing excited by this new adventure.

The clerk, instead of diving for the alarm button when Kendrick entered, smiled widely at the cubs and pointed out the way to the bathrooms. He was helpful to the kids when they were trying to decide what junk food they wanted to eat, and didn't charge them for the extra soda when Robbie spilled his.

The clerk rang up the purchases, took Kendrick's cash, said a cheerful good night to the cubs, and that was it.

The way it should be, Kendrick thought as he helped the cubs carry the food back to the motorcycle. *No Collars to signal we're different. No restrictions, no fear. The guy didn't even know we weren't the same as him.*

Kendrick got the cubs settled in again, the bags of food tucked around them. They'd drive on and find somewhere in the wild to camp and eat.

He straightened up, preparing to walk the bike to a darker patch where he could strap on the sword again. Then he froze, hackles rising.

A man, a Shifter, stood right in front of him. He wore a leather coat against the growing cold, had dark hair peppered with gray at his temples, and blue eyes that went fathoms down. The neckline of his shirt just hid the gleam of a silver Collar.

"Kendrick Shaughnessy," Dylan Morrissey said. "We need to talk."

CHAPTER NINETEEN

Rebecca woke in her own bed at home. She stared, puzzled, at sunlight playing on the ceiling, familiar shadows from the trees outside dancing to greet her.

She moved, thinking she needed to get up and start breakfast, but a stab of pain sent her right back down. She groaned, gritting her teeth as waves of agony rolled over her.

The door opened, and the worried faces of Cherie and Olaf peeked around it. Rebecca regarded them without reaction for a moment, then she relaxed, her body knowing it was home, and gestured for them to come in.

"What happened to me?" she asked in a weak voice. "I must have drunk a hell of a lot to have this hangover."

Even as she spoke, the events of the night soared back at her—everything from leaving here with Walker, his face painted in groupie makeup, to dragging him out from under the rubble and collapsing with him in the dirt outside the compound.

"Is Walker all right?" she asked in alarm. "Where is he?"

"He went home," Olaf said, regarding her with his still, dark eyes. "He said we had to take care of you."

"Oh." Well, what had she expected? That she'd wake up with him next to her, holding her hand? Walker had his own world, his own life. The mission was over.

"You were hurt worse than he was," Cherie said, sitting carefully on the edge of the bed. "He said he was going to get patched up. You had a broken leg, but Andrea healed you."

Rebecca tentatively moved her right leg. It ached like crazy, but the pain she'd felt at the compound had gone.

Andrea, a half Fae, half Shifter, had the gift of healing magic. Rebecca was grateful to her but just as happy to have been passed out for the treatment. Her bones melding back together couldn't have felt good.

She struggled to sit up, finding that someone had put her into the long T-shirt she liked to sleep in. Cherie laid a concerned hand on her unhurt leg.

"Andrea says you should stay in bed a while longer. Elizabeth and Ronan said so too."

"No, no. I need to get up. Things to do." Rebecca sucked in a sharp breath and ended up slumped against the bed's headboard. "Then again, maybe later."

Scott chose that moment to walk in, a steaming cup in his hand. "I thought you might like some coffee."

Rebecca inhaled the fragrant aroma and held out both hands. "Gimme. Thank you."

Scott set the mug between her reaching fingers. Rebecca noticed as she took a pull of the wonderful brew that he was quieter, less restless this morning—even polite and thoughtful. For the first time in a long time, he looked comfortable in his own skin. Maybe his Transition was truly over.

Rebecca swallowed the coffee, already feeling better. "So is anyone going to fill me in on what happened after I passed out?"

Scott and Cherie started talking at once, until Scott let Cherie glare him to silence.

"Ronan says that Dylan got the alert from Walker," Cherie said. "I guess Dylan was waiting for it, because he rounded up everyone and led them out. They found an underground compound down south of San Antonio and some Shifters with no Collars. A lot of the Shifters got away, but a few were rounded up."

"What about Nancy? Joanne's sister?"

"She's with Joanne at Broderick's," Cherie went on. "So is Aleck, the Shifter Nancy was with. I guess Broderick's family is going to look after both of them. Nancy agreed to report herself not missing so the police will stop looking for her, but Aleck isn't going to be turned in. Nancy's carrying his cub." Cherie made the last announcement with a look of triumph. She loved being the first to spread such news.

"Wow." Rebecca took another sip of coffee. She loved the stuff so much. "No wonder they didn't want to let each other go. Not what I was expecting."

Cherie nodded. "That's what Ronan said."

"What about Kendrick? The Guardian? Did they find him?" Rebecca frowned thoughtfully, cradling the mug. "And what the heck is a Guardian doing leading Shifters? That's not what they do."

Scott answered this time. "Ronan didn't say much about him. Neither did Broderick, except things like *fucked up, crazy-ass Guardian Shifter with delusions of grandeur—Goddess save me from another effing tiger.* Dylan's still out, but he sent word he wants to keep it quiet that there's Collar-less Shifters running around. Walker, before he left, said he wouldn't tell."

"Walker's Shifter Bureau," Rebecca said. "It's his job to tell."

"Nah," Scott said with confidence. "Walker's cool."

"Walker would never tell," Olaf said. "He promised me."

And that was good enough for Olaf. As he hoisted himself up onto the bed beside Rebecca, she noted that his thin legs were a bit longer than they used to be. The little cub was growing up. Rebecca put her arm around Olaf and snuggled him close.

"I guess we'll find out," Rebecca said, pressing a kiss to Olaf's white hair. "When he comes back."

Except that Walker didn't come back.

———

REBECCA'S LEG FINISHED HEALING OVER THE NEXT couple days, as did the rest of her fighting wounds. Her strong Shifter metabolism quickly bounced her back into good health.

As she grew stronger, her restlessness returned, more intense than usual. No word came from Walker, which made her crankier by the day. She tried to settle in and enjoy looking after the cubs, cooking meals with Elizabeth, going with Ronan to Liam's bar, hanging out with friends, but she ended up growly and unhappy.

Rebecca wasn't a woman to wait by the phone for a man to call her. She carried her phone around with her instead, pretending not to glance at it twenty times a day to make sure she hadn't missed Walker's call.

She needed to go out and run, but Rebecca remembered what had happened the last time she'd done that. She was tired of getting knocked out and waking up in cells. She didn't even know whether she was still restricted by her house arrest. Walker could have at least told her that, or told Ronan, if he didn't want to talk to her. She'd glare at the phone and will it to ring.

Meanwhile, Nancy and Aleck settled into Broderick's big house. There was talk of putting a Collar on Aleck to see if that would help keep him from going feral, but so far, no one wanted to attempt it. Taking a Collar was a painful experience, and no one wanted to subject the poor guy—and by extension, Nancy—to that.

Dylan had brought in the young Tevis as well, plus a few other Shifters he'd captured, most of them relatively young and too inexperienced to evade competent trackers like Spike, Ellison, and most especially, Tiger. A lot of meetings happened at the Morrissey house about how to deal with the problem of the un-Collared Shifters.

Dylan said nothing at all about Kendrick. The tacit understanding was that Kendrick had survived but was in the wind. Rebecca had caught Dylan's scent when he'd explained this to her and Ronan—he wasn't exactly lying, but not telling the whole truth either. Dylan was up to something, but unless he wanted Rebecca to know about it, she'd never find out what.

Five days after their adventure, Rebecca banged out onto the porch, ill at ease. It was hot that afternoon, the temp about ninety—as could happen in Austin even in late October. Tomorrow, on the other hand, it could drop into the forties, so she decided to enjoy the sunshine by pulling on a pair of cutoff shorts and going barefoot. It had taken Rebecca a long time to adjust to living in a warm climate, but she embraced it now.

The door to the Den opened, and Walker strode out.

Rebecca paused a split second then slowed her quick stride and strolled down the porch steps to the cool grass, meeting Walker in the middle of the lawn.

The words *Where the hell have you been?* died on her lips. She would not be a shrew, she told herself, and she would not give him the satisfaction of knowing she'd been pining for him.

"Oh, hey, Walker." Rebecca forced her voice to be light. "I didn't know you were here."

"Just arrived." Sunlight glistened on his buzzed hair, his hard, muscular arms, the cool blue of his eyes. He was in what she called his casual fatigues—black pants and boots, black T-shirt stretching across his chest.

He didn't ask if she were all right. Obviously Rebecca was whole and walking around, and he could easily have found out how she was doing from Ronan or anyone else in this house. They didn't hold back.

Rebecca put one hand on her hip, looking straight into his eyes, challenging him. He stared right back at her. When she'd first met him, Walker had been a little nervous around her, not always making eye contact.

Not anymore. But then, they'd been on a harrowing mission together, had shared burning kisses, intimate moments in the dark, not to mention saving each other's lives.

Walker looked her over without shyness now. He took in the swell of her breasts under her V-necked white T-shirt, the jeans shorts just covering her butt, and her long legs with the remnants of scars from the fight in the compound.

He took his time, then finally gave her a brief nod. "Come on into the Den."

Why? So they could discuss her arrest? The outcome of the mission? What to do with the un-Collared Shifters?

Rebecca made a casual flip of her hand, indicating he should lead on. Walker turned and strode into the dim interior of the Den, not hurrying, but not waiting for her either. Rebecca hesitated a few heartbeats, then she scurried across the lawn and inside after him, banging the door shut behind her.

CHAPTER TWENTY

Walker liked that Rebecca had made sure the door closed all the way, shutting them in together. She wanted to be alone with him, no matter that she probably wanted the privacy to yell at him. Never mind, she'd look hotter than hell when she did it.

Had she dressed this way today to mess with his head? No, she hadn't known he was coming. Walker had sworn Ronan to secrecy.

He hadn't had a real relationship for so long that he'd forgotten one rule. Women might claim that they liked being surprised, but they didn't, not really.

Too late now.

Rebecca halted inside the door and stared around her. "What's all this?"

Open boxes, half unpacked, rested in various places in the room. The banner from the army company Walker had been assigned to hung on one wall. It was always the first thing he put up when he moved into a new place.

"My stuff," Walker said. "I cleared out of my apartment."

She didn't move. "I thought you lived on the post at Shifter Bureau."

"They don't have much housing there. I had an apartment instead—a crappy one. This will be more comfortable." He looked around what had once been a three-car garage. "And bigger."

"Wait, wait, wait." Rebecca waved her open hands. "You're moving in?"

"Spent the last couple days packing up and paying my way out of my lease. Plus writing up the mission and turning in paperwork." Walker had taken his time writing his report, choosing what got made official and what was left out. He'd left a lot of things out.

Walker moved a pile of his shirts from the bed and dropped them into the drawer of a big dresser.

"*Why* are you moving in?" Rebecca didn't come any closer or give him a warm, happy look—nothing like that.

Walker shut the drawer. "I figured I might as well."

"So you can liaise with Shifters?"

"Something like that." Walker turned and moved slowly toward her. Rebecca watched him come, remaining in place, saying nothing.

Walker reached her. In her bare feet, she was the same height as he was, and they looked into each other's eyes.

Instead of the cockiness and irritation he expected to find, Walker read uncertainty, even fear in her expression, along with determination not to show it.

Walker had never been an eloquent man. He couldn't seduce a woman with sexy phrases, because he didn't know any. He only knew how to shut up and get on with his life, or how to tell the stark truth. So, he opted for stark truth.

"I'm here because I want to be with you," he said.

Rebecca's chest rose with a sharp intake of breath. Walker stepped closer, sliding his hands to her waist. Under the soft fabric of her shirt, she was warm, supple.

"Remember when I said I wanted to make love to you?" Walker asked.

Rebecca gave him the tiniest nod.

"I said that we'd finish the mission," he continued, "then find a mattress and some privacy."

"I remember." Her voice was the barest whisper.

"There's a mattress over there. And we have privacy. Relatively." The Den was ten yards from a large house full of Shifters, all of them nosy.

A swallow moved down her throat. "That's true."

Walker caressed her waist. He felt her shiver—Rebecca, the confident, sexy woman who dropped Shifters with one flash of her eyes, was nervous, shy with him.

That was a good thing.

He slowly slid his hands beneath the shirt, carefully peeling it from her sides and upward. Rebecca stood still and let him push her shirt off over her head, her dark hair tumbling around her shoulders.

She was bare underneath, nothing to fetter her breasts, which nestled into his hands.

She was sublimely beautiful. No thin, underfed woman Walker feared he'd break, but a large, gorgeous, strong lady with lush breasts and eyes he could drown in.

He leaned forward as she drew another breath, and caught her lips, easing her mouth open to taste her.

She made a sound in her throat, and her hands came up, gripping his shoulders. As Walker deepened the kiss, Rebecca dragged his shirt up, baring his chest and back to the warm air.

He eased away from her to yank the shirt all the way off and toss it aside. Then he stepped to her again, cupping her face, the next kiss hotter and fuller.

Every hesitation, every inhibition they'd had with each other fell away, layer by layer, warmth and need taking over. In another moment, they were pressed together, Rebecca's breasts to his chest, her hands on his back.

Walker slid his fingers from her face to the back of her neck, scooping her to him. She tasted of fire, of the heat of the day, the spice of her wildness.

He didn't want a woman who said, *Yes, dear,* and laid out his clothes for him—Walker wanted exotic Rebecca to lie with in the dark of the night, to laugh with when they figured out breakfast in the morning. He wanted her sly smile, her teasing, her strength, and her love.

When the kiss ended, they were both breathless, each holding the other as hard as Aleck and Nancy had held hands. Both hungry.

The bed contained a pile of folded sheets and blankets. Walker shoved them off in one sweep, and popped the button of Rebecca's waistband, loosening the tiny shorts.

The cutoffs fell easily, and Walker's hands sank into her sweet, bare buttocks. She'd gone commando underneath.

His grin stretched his face. "You're a bad, bad woman."

Rebecca gave him an innocent look. "What? It's hot. And besides . . ." Walker's blood started to boil as she slanted him that sexy smile. "You might have come over."

"I'm glad I did."

"Me too," she said in a soft voice, and bit his lower lip.

Walker growled a growl worthy of any Shifter, and made quick work of getting rid of his own pants and underwear. She was bare now, nothing between her and him. Their press of bodies as he kissed her again was hotter than the day outside.

Rebecca broke away and stepped back, but only to look him up and down. "My, my," she said, her gaze blatantly taking him in. "That was worth the wait."

"I'm tired of waiting," Walker said. "Come here."

He didn't like not having his arms around her. Walker entwined her again and guided her down to the bed.

Rebecca was worth looking at in return. He'd already seen her naked several times—including on the first day he'd met her—but her stripping to shift and stripping to go to bed with him were entirely different things.

Her skin was flushed, her breasts tight, the dark points of her areolas betraying that she was as needy as he was. Walker had nothing to hide. She knew he wanted her, and her gaze moved to the stiff cock that rose higher as she studied it.

Walker moved above Rebecca on hands and knees, her body open and welcoming. He kissed her as he lay down on her, her arms enfolding him.

The next kiss seared him to the bone. Rebecca pulled him close, her softness like a drug. Walker inhaled her warm scent, licked across her lips, bent the leg she hadn't hurt, and slid himself inside her.

Perfect.

Rebecca dragged in a breath, her head going back, her

hair moving on the mattress. Walker smothered a groan as her heat enclosed him.

Then he was moving, unable to hold back, unable to go slowly. He'd wanted this woman from the moment he'd met her. She pulled him to her now, her kisses fierce, her body rising to his.

Walker thrust, and Rebecca met him. They gave up on being quiet at the same time, Rebecca's cries blending with Walker's deeper ones as they moved faster and faster.

The overhead fan that wafted air to Walker's back couldn't cut the heat. Their bodies were slick, sliding against each other's, Rebecca's fingers hard points in his back.

She wasn't gentle with him, nor he with her. They both needed someone with strength, someone who could understand the other's restless energy, and both take it and give back.

Well matched, ran through Walker's head, but it really wasn't a coherent thought.

His body had taken over, his brain shutting off, and all Walker knew was the soft delight of Rebecca and the incandescent feeling of thrusting inside her. He could stay here forever, with her hands pulling him to her, her mouth seeking his kisses.

Walker had done enough for the world. Time for the world to go the hell away.

Rebecca's cries grew louder, until she rose hard against him, coming apart, her joy breaking something open inside him.

Too soon, all too soon, he was coming with her, their shouts ringing through the room.

Rebecca smiled, breathless, as Walker collapsed on top

of her, and they gathered each other in for slow, afterglow, very fine kisses.

The simple lines of the Den, with the scattered, open boxes, piles of clothes to put away, and the bare mattress had become the most beautiful place in the world.

———

REBECCA DROWSED IN THE SUNSHINE POURING THROUGH the window a long time later, snuggling up to Walker on the unmade bed. Sunlight caught the rough gold on his jaw and brushed his strong hand resting on her hip. Walker's body was nothing but muscle, a man who kept himself in fighting shape.

Rebecca smoothed her fingers over his cheek, and he opened his eyes. He blinked a moment, coming out of sleep, then he smiled.

The smile pierced Rebecca to the heart. "What do we do now?" she whispered.

"I don't know," he said, grin broadening. "I liked what we did when I was lying behind you. I'm willing to try that again."

Rebecca had to laugh, and agree it had been fun. "You know what I mean. Mating for Shifters is different. It's not only the ceremony, it's—"

"The mate bond. I know." Walker ran his hand up her side then down her arm to twine her fingers with his. "Are you afraid you won't feel it with me?"

"I'm afraid I will." Afraid she already did. "What happens to me then?"

"Humans can feel it too," Walker said. He tugged Rebecca's hand to his chest and pressed it there. "It's been hot and tingling inside for a while now. You think that's what it is?"

Rebecca sat up abruptly, her heart beating faster. "And you didn't say anything?"

"We've been busy." Walker gave her another warm flash of the smile that always got to her. "I figured when it was time to talk, we would."

"Time like now?"

Walker shrugged, the ripple running the length of his naked body. "Good a time as any. A little bit from now, I'm not going to want to talk anymore."

"Yeah?" Rebecca let herself relax, insane happiness threatening to take over. "What are you going to want to do?"

"Something we'll both have fun figuring out."

Other parts of Rebecca besides her heart began to burn. "Talking's overrated," she said. "You can talk things to death."

"That's true. But there's some things I think we should say." Walker took her hand again, wrapping his fingers firmly around hers. "I like immersion. Whenever I'm sent to a new country, a new culture, and have to figure out how to work in it, I plunge myself deep into that culture. I eat the food, speak the language, read what they read, listen to what they talk about, figure out what's important to them. You know what I've learned?"

"New recipes?" Rebecca asked.

Walker's chuckle jostled her. "That people are pretty much the same the world over. We all have different traditions, sometimes different sets of values, but deep down, it's more the same than different. They worry about their kids and how to provide for their families; they value the people they care about—friends, family. I meet bad people who do terrible things, but I also meet good people who genuinely care. But for the most part, we're all just struggling to get through the day."

"Makes sense," Rebecca answered, distracted by the heat of his palm against hers. "And?"

"If I'm going to find out what it's like to be a Shifter mate, I need total immersion. With you, your family, the cubs, other Shifters. No long-distance relationships. They don't work well for me until they stop being long-distance."

"You only lived halfway across town," Rebecca pointed out.

"Halfway across town but in a different world. I'm going to stay in this one awhile." Walker's eyes twinkled, like a sudden beam of sunshine on silver blue waters. "Get used to it."

Rebecca's heart beat faster. "What happens once you're all the way immersed?"

Another shrug, another hot shift of muscles. "We ask Liam to do the mating ceremonies. Or you kick my ass. I'm willing to see which one happens first."

Rebecca sent him a wide smile. "You think I can kick your ass?"

"Sure. You're pretty good at sparring. Plus, you have that whole Kodiak Shifter thing going for you. I know what it's like now to be shaken awake by a giant bear. Won't forget that in a hurry. I was glad you were on my side."

Rebecca's smile deepened, the warmth of it reaching down her body. "When you were throwing around that arsenal, I was glad you were on mine."

"I learned to be surprising."

"That's good," Rebecca said.

"Yeah?" Walker looked thoughtful. "When I brought you in here this afternoon, I had the feeling you didn't like surprises."

"That was different." She cupped his cheek. "If I learn to expect your surprises, I'll never be bored."

He frowned. "If you expect them, they won't be surprises."

Rebecca leaned to him, unable to stay away any longer. "Then I'll have to come up with some surprises of my own."

"Yeah? Well, I've been trained to pretty much not be surprised."

"Hmm." Rebecca lay quietly against him for a moment, then she slammed her legs around his and flipped him in a sudden, practiced move.

And found herself being flipped again, Walker landing on top of her, pinning her wrists to the mattress.

"Surprise," he said.

"Want to bet?" Rebecca squirmed, breaking his hold, and rolled out from under him, but he came after her.

Walker did know neat, precise, and unexpected moves that turned the wrestling match into a victory for him.

But she'd learn, Rebecca thought as she lay panting beneath him. He'd won . . . but had he really? She had a hot, hard-bodied man on top of her, and no doubt about what was on his mind.

Walker looked down at her, his grin fading as warmth entered his eyes. "Hey, Becks," he said softly.

"Yeah?" Her hands were trapped under his, and she had no intention of struggling free.

Walker leaned down, breath hot on her skin, and whispered into her ear. "I love you."

Rebecca turned her head so they were nose-to-nose, she never more willing to lose a fight in her life. The magic in her heart burned and sang. "I love you too."

Walker released her to cup her face, pulling her to him to kiss her deeply. Rebecca surrendered to the kiss, then came out of surrender and started to kiss him back, touching him in return. Sparring in a different way.

Walker's smile came back as he eased away, both of them catching their breaths. "I like this. Total immersion in being in love."

"It's not bad so far," Rebecca said.

Walker came in closer, his body the length of hers. "I'll have to stay here a good long while."

Rebecca brushed her fingers through his hair, liking the feel of it. "Good," she said, and smiled up at her mate. "In that case, welcome to my home."

"Glad to be here," Walker said, then he slid back inside her until they were one. Complete.

ALSO BY JENNIFER ASHLEY

Shifters Unbound

Pride Mates

Primal Bonds

Bodyguard

Wild Cat

Hard Mated

Mate Claimed

"Perfect Mate" (novella)

Lone Wolf

Tiger Magic

Feral Heat

Wild Wolf

Bear Attraction

Mate Bond

Lion Eyes

Bad Wolf

Wild Things

White Tiger

Guardian's Mate

Red Wolf

Midnight Wolf

Tiger Striped

A Shifter Christmas Carol

Iron Master

The Last Warrior

Tiger's Daughter

Bear Facts

Stray Cat

Shifter Made ("Prequel" novella)

Stormwalker Series (w/a Allyson James)

Stormwalker

Firewalker

Shadow Walker

"Double Hexed"

Nightwalker

Dreamwalker

Dragon Bites

Wing Dancer

Shape Changer

SHIFTERS UNBOUND
SERIES BY SHIFTERTOWN

Austin Shifters
Pride Mates (Liam and Kim)
Primal Bonds (Sean and Andrea)
Bodyguard (Ronan and Elizabeth)
Hard Mated (Spike and Myka)
Lone Wolf (Ellison and Maria)
Tiger Magic (Tiger and Carly:
Tiger first appears in *Mate Claimed*, Las Vegas Shifters)
Feral Heat (Deni and Jace.
Jace crosses over from the Las Vegas Shifters)
Bear Attraction (Walker and Rebecca.
Crosses over to Kendrick's group)
Bad Wolf (Broderick and Joanne.
Briefly crosses with Montana Shiftertown)
Wild Things (Mason and Jasmine.
Intro of haunted house and Zander)
Tiger Striped (Tiger and Carly novella)
A Shifter Christmas Carol

(novella featuring Dylan)
The Last Warrior (Ben and Rhianne)
(Ben crosses over to other Shiftertowns)
Tiger's Daughter (Connor and Tiger-Girl)

Kendrick's Group
(Most cross over with Austin Shifters)
Lion Eyes (Seamus and Bree)
White Tiger (Kendrick and Addison)
Red Wolf (Jaycee and Dimitri)

Las Vegas Shifters
Wild Cat (Cassidy and Diego)
Mate Claimed (Eric and Iona)
Perfect Mate (Nell and Cormac)
Wild Wolf (Graham and Misty)
Iron Master (Stuart Reid and Peigi)
Bear Facts (Shane and Freya)
Stray Cat (Xav and Lindsay)

North Carolina Shifters
Mate Bond (Bowman and Kenzie.
Crossover with Las Vegas Shifters)

New Orleans Shifters
Midnight Wolf (Angus and Tamsin.
Crosses over with Austin Shifters and Zander)

Montana Shifters
Guardian's Mate (Zander and Rae)

ABOUT THE AUTHOR

New York Times bestselling and award-winning author Jennifer Ashley has more than 120 published novels and novellas in mystery, romance, historical fiction, and urban fantasy under the names Jennifer Ashley, Allyson James, and Ashley Gardner. Jennifer's books have been translated into more than a dozen languages and have earned starred reviews in *Publisher's Weekly* and *Booklist*. When she isn't writing, Jennifer enjoys playing music (guitar, piano, flute), reading, hiking, cooking, and building dollhouse miniatures.

More about Jennifer's books can be found at
http://www.jenniferashley.com

To keep up to date on her new releases, join her newsletter here:
http://eepurl.com/47kLL